MYTHS AND LEGENDS

THESEUS AND THE MINOTAUR

BY GRAEME DAVIS
ILLUSTRATED BY JOSÉ DANIEL CABRERA PEÑA

First published in Great Britain in 2014 by Osprey Publishing,
Kemp House, Chawley Park, Cumnor Hill, Oxford, OX2 9PH, UK
4301 21st. St., Suite 220, Long Island City, NY 11101, USA
E-mail: info@ospreypublishing.com

Osprey Publishing is part of the Osprey Group

A CIP catalog record for this book is available from the British Library

Print ISBN: 978 1 4728 0405 1
PDF e-book ISBN: 978 1 4728 0407 5
EPUB e-book ISBN: 978 1 4728 0406 8

Typeset in Garamond Pro and Myriad Pro

Originated by PDQ Media, Bungay, UK
Printed in China through Asia Pacific Offset Ltd.

14 15 16 17 18   10 9 8 7 6 5 4 3 2 1

Osprey Publishing is supporting the Woodland Trust, the UK's leading woodland conservation charity, by funding the dedication of trees.

www.ospreypublishing.com

CONTENTS

INTRODUCTION

The story of Theseus and the Minotaur is one of the best-known Greek myths. It has inspired plays, films, books, and countless fantasy games. The Minotaur, originally a unique monster, has spawned an entire race of bull-headed ogres in games like *Dungeons & Dragons*. But the slaying of the Minotaur is only one part of an entire cycle of tales recounting Theseus' adventures.

Born with divine blood, Theseus' youthful adventures mirror the spread of Athenian influence through the surrounding region of Attica. He is said to have traveled with Hercules, battled the Amazons, sailed with the Argonauts, and kidnapped a youthful Helen in the years before the Trojan War. As king of Athens, he enacted reforms that laid the foundation for Athenian democracy.

The historical Theseus, if there was one, seems to have lived at some time between 1300 and 1200 BC. A generation before the Trojan War, this was a pivotal time in Greek history, when history was only just beginning to emerge from the mists of mythology. The land of Greece, dominated by the Mycenaean and Minoan cultures of the late Bronze Age, was beginning to take its first steps toward the Classical era.

An illustration of Plutarch. His *Life of Theseus* is the most detailed ancient source for the hero's story. (Alamy)

Sources

As well as being among the best-known Greek myths, the adventures of Theseus are also among the most retold. Each version differs from all the others, and there is no single authoritative text. The two principal sources are the *Life of Theseus* by the first-century Greek writer Plutarch and the *Metamorphoses* by the Roman poet Ovid. Each writer has his own strengths and weaknesses.

Plutarch is considered by some to be the father of modern biography. He is careful to record as many different versions of a tale as he can, and he makes reference to many earlier historians whose work are now lost. His *Life of Theseus* is thorough, but his digressions into alternative sources and versions can make it difficult to read.

Ovid's *Metamorphoses* collect over 250 myths into 15 books, united by the overall theme of love and its power to make fools even of the gods. The adventures of Theseus are found in the seventh book, and are retold in a highly poetic style that can also be hard to follow.

In addition, certain episodes from Theseus' life and adventures – especially the deaths of his wife Phaedra and son Hippolytus – were popular with Greek and Roman tragedians, each of whom told a slightly different version of the story.

The purpose of this book is to collect together information from a wide range of contradictory sources and organize it as clearly as possible without losing the diversity represented by the different versions. It also seeks to set the stories in their historical contexts – the times they represent and the times in which they were written down – and to show how they might reflect actual Bronze Age events that have been established by historians and archeologists.

Theseus and the Metaphor

The story of Theseus is set in a kind of dreamtime where history and mythology overlap. Although the tale has many elements that are pure myth, it is also thought that it contains echoes of historical truth, albeit in a highly mythologized and allegorical form.

The earliest surviving sources for the story of Theseus date to the Classical era, when Athens was the undisputed mistress of Greece. While Theseus is not credited with founding the city as Romulus is with founding Rome, he is still the greatest Athenian hero and an allegorical embodiment of the city's might and destiny, seen by the Athenians in much the same light as medieval Britons regarded the legendary King Arthur. The myths of Theseus can be read at face value as a series of adventure stories, or they can be seen as an allegory for the early spread of Athenian influence in an age dominated by the Minoan and Mycenaean cultures.

The Age of Theseus

Most classical sources place the life of Theseus between 1273 BC and *c.* 1223 BC, a generation before the Trojan War. Theseus' sons Demophon and Acamas were said to have been among the warriors who hid in the famous Trojan Horse.

Late Minoan IIIC

In Crete, archeologists call this period Late Minoan IIIC. It marks the final phase of the Minoan civilization, and is marked by the widespread destruction by fire of Minoan palaces on Crete and Mycenaean palaces on the Greek mainland. The events surrounding the destruction are unclear, and theories include civil strife or invasion by the Dorian Greeks or the mysterious Sea Peoples who attacked across the eastern Mediterranean at this time.

Theseus and the Minotaur by Etienne-Jules Ramey, 1826. Tuileries Gardens, Paris. (Photograph by Thesupermat)

The Sea Peoples are also credited with destroying the Hittite Empire in Anatolia and the Mitanni civilization of southern Anatolia and northern Syria at about this time, and with attacking Egypt in the reign of Ramses III. However, they are not mentioned in any of the Theseus myths.

The Dorian Greeks are said by some ancient writers to be the descendants of Hercules, who returned to Greece after several generations in exile. Given that Theseus and Hercules are said to have adventured together, it seems that this must have taken place well after Theseus' time. In light of a dearth of hard evidence for a distinctive Dorian people, some modern archeologists believe that the "Dorian invasion" was invented in the 19th century to explain the collapse of the Minoan and Mycenaean civilizations. Even if these people did exist, the Dorian invasion does not figure in any of the Theseus myths, and it is unlikely that such a significant historical event would have gone unmentioned.

It is also worth noting that the victims of this destruction were Mycenaean Greeks rather than Minoans. The Greeks had occupied Crete and taken over its palaces around 1420 BC, following an earlier disaster that for some signals the end of "pure" Minoan culture.

FROM MYTH TO HISTORY

It might be argued that the Trojan War marks a dividing line between the age of Greek myth and the dawn of Greek history. Homer's account of the war was once thought to be nothing more than a legend, but since the 19th-century German archeologist Heinrich Schliemann discovered the ruins of a great Bronze Age city near the village of Hisarlik in western Turkey, it has been generally agreed that the Trojan War was a real historical event.

Although all accounts agree that Theseus lived before the Trojan War, he is still one of the latest of the Greek heroes, and to some extent he reflects his times. Gods no longer walk the earth, and their meddling in mortal affairs is positively restrained by Olympian standards. Theseus' adventures provide a link between the Age of Greek Mythology and the Classical era of Greek History, underpinning historical events such as the rise of Athens to regional prominence and the last days of the Minoan-Mycenaean cultural complex that had dominated the eastern Mediterranean in the late Bronze Age.

As might be expected, then, the surviving accounts are a mix of mythic adventure and early history. Like Jason, Theseus was a hero who walked in two worlds. Despite the overtly fantastic nature of some of his adventures, he is perhaps the most likely of all the Greek heroes to have actually lived.

THESEUS' EARLY LIFE

Theseus had two fathers, one mortal and one immortal. His mother, Aethra, was a princess from the city of Troezen, across the Saronic Gulf to the southwest of Athens.

Aegeus

Aegeus, the king of Athens, had been married twice, but was still childless. He went to consult the oracle of Delphi, but received a very puzzling answer: "Do not loosen the bulging mouth of the wineskin until you have reached the height of Athens, lest you die of grief." He had no idea what to make of it.

King Pittheus of Troezen was renowned for his skill at interpreting oracles, and Aegeus visited Troezen to consult him. Pittheus introduced Aegeus to his daughter Aethra, and the two spent a drunken night together. The same night, Athena came to Aethra in a dream and prompted her to wade to the nearby island of Sphairia, where she was visited by the god Poseidon in the form of a bull. There is some disagreement as to the order of these two liaisons, but, in any event, Theseus was conceived with a mixture of mortal and divine blood.

Before leaving the pregnant Aethra and returning to Athens, Aegeus buried his sword and his sandals under a huge rock. He told her that when her child was strong enough to lift the rock and take them, he should come to Athens. Aegeus cautioned Aethra that secrecy was vital; a powerful faction of nobles called the Pallantides, or sons of Pallas, coveted the throne of Athens, and the child would be in grave danger if they discovered he was Aegeus' heir.

Theseus lifts the stone to take his father's sword in this Roman terracotta from the second century AD. (Ancient Art & Architecture Collection Ltd / Alamy)

Aegeus consults the Oracle in this vase painting from the fifth century BC. Currently held in the Altes Museum, Berlin

Theseus was raised at his grandfather's court in Troezen. To protect him, Pittheus concealed his connection with Aegeus and spread the half-truth that Theseus was a son of Poseidon, for whom the people of Troezen had a particular reverence.

One incident in his childhood showed that Theseus was destined to be a hero. The great Hercules came to visit Troezen after completing his famous labors. Taking off the skin of the Nemean Lion, which he wore as a cloak, Hercules laid it on a couch, where it sat in a most lifelike manner. The other children were terrified, but Theseus picked up an axe and attacked the supposed monster.

The Journey to Athens

When Theseus was grown, his mother showed him the stone under which Aegeus had left his sword and sandals. Theseus lifted the stone easily and took the gifts that his mortal father had left him. His mother and grandfather advised him to travel to Athens by sea; the journey was both shorter and safer. However, Theseus decided that he would take the longer and more dangerous land route, braving bandits and other dangers along the way.

Periphetes the Clubber

Soon after leaving his mother and grandfather, Theseus passed by the small city of Epidaurus. It was renowned as the birthplace of the healing god Asclepius, and its great *Asclepeion* or healing temple attracted pilgrims from across Greece. It was close to Epidaurus that Theseus encountered the bandit known as Periphetes the Clubber.

Like Theseus, Periphetes was half-divine. His father was the smith-god Hephaestus, and, like his father, Periphetes was lame in one leg but possessed prodigious strength. He had only one eye, in the middle of his head, just like the Cyclops that helped his father with his forge. For many years, Periphetes had killed unwary travelers with his great bronze club, driving his victims into the ground like fence-posts.

When Periphetes attacked Theseus, the hero dodged the mighty club, grabbed the end of it, and yanked it out of Periphetes' hands. He then used it to beat Periphetes into the ground, as Periphetes had done to so many innocent travelers. Theseus kept the bronze club and carried it in many of his later adventures.

OPPOSITE
Periphetes was Theseus' first opponent as a hero. He tricked the notorious robber and killed him with his own bronze club.

Sinis the Pine Bender

Leaving Epidaurus behind, Theseus soon reached the Isthmus of Corinth, the narrow strip of land that connects the Peloponnesus, the southern portion of Greece, to the mainland in the north. It was here that Theseus encountered his second foe, Sinis the Pine Bender.

FUNERAL GAMES

The most famous athletic event of the ancient world was the Olympic Games, which is said to have started in 776 BC as a religious festival in honor of Zeus. Funeral games are an older custom, and some scholars believe that the Olympic Games grew out of this tradition.

One of the earliest mentions of ancient Greek sports is found in Homer's *Iliad*. Achilles, the greatest of the Greek warriors, honors the shade of his fallen kinsman Patroclus with animal and human sacrifices and a set of funeral games that include foot and chariot races, discus and javelin throwing, and wrestling, archery, and sword-fighting contests.

Ancient sources suggest that funeral games were common in Mycenaean Greece and other ancient cultures. The Etruscan and early Roman civilizations also held games to honor the dead, but as time passed their emphasis shifted more and more toward bloodshed and spectacle, ending in the gladiatorial games for which Rome became notorious.

Unlike Theseus and Periphetes, Sinis was entirely mortal. He was a grandson of Corinthus, the king of Corinth. Sinis tricked passing travelers into helping him bend a pine tree to the ground, and while his victim was occupied he would suddenly lash his wrists to the tree and let it go, hurling his hapless victim to his death.

When Sinis saw Theseus approaching, he called out to the young man to come and help him with the tree he was bending. Theseus ran up, grabbed hold of the tree top, and helped pull it to the ground. However, when Sinis sprang at him and tried to tie his hand to the tree, Theseus caught the killer and tied his hand to the pine tree instead. Then, still holding Sinis, Theseus bent a second pine and tied the killer's other hand to that one. When Theseus let go of both trees, they sprang upright, tearing Sinis in half.

As the muderer died, Theseus heard a scream behind him and saw a young woman run and hide in a bed of rushes and asparagus. Theseus eventually coaxed the woman out, promising not to harm her, and discovered that she was Perigune, the daughter of Sinis. Grateful to be free of her murderous father, Perigune slept with Theseus. The next morning, Theseus continued on his way, but many months later Perigune gave birth to his son, Melanippus.

The Crommyonian Sow

Between Corinth and Megara lay the village of Crommyon. For many months, the surrounding area had been ravaged by a wild monstrous pig. The sow had killed so many of the farmers that they no longer went out to plow their fields, and the village was on the edge of ruin. When Theseus reached Crommyon, he heard of the villagers' plight, so he hunted down the sow and killed it, thus saving the village.

Sciron

Theseus continued on his way. As the road neared the city of Megara, it ran along the edge of a steep cliff called the Scironian Rocks. This was the haunt of an elderly bandit named Sciron, who was another son of the sea-god, Poseidon. Whenever lone travelers came down the road, Sciron would stop them and demand that they wash his feet. However, when they knelt down to do so, Sciron would kick them off the cliff into the ocean, where they would be devoured by a monstrous turtle.

When Sciron demanded that Theseus wash his feet, the young hero readily agreed. However, when the aged bandit tried to kick him over the cliff, Theseus caught his foot and hurled him off the rocks into the ocean below. From the top of the cliff, Theseus watched as the great turtle tore the murderous bandit to pieces.

Many years later, Theseus created the Isthmian Games to atone for this kinslaying, since Sciron was another son of Poseidon.

Cercyon

When Theseus was only 12 miles from Athens, he passed the town of Eleusis, which was famous as the home of the Eleusinian mysteries, a cult of Demeter and Persephone.

Cercyon, the king of Eleusis, haunted the roads around Eleusis and challenged passers-by to a wrestling-match, promising his kingdom to any opponent who could defeat him. He was undefeated when Theseus met him, having killed everyone who dared to fight him by crushing them in a mighty bear hug.

Theseus agreed to the match, knowing he could rely on his skill to overcome Cercyon's brute strength. When the mad king came at him, Theseus dodged out of his crushing

Theseus battles the Crommyonian Sow in this fifth-century BC terracotta plaque from the island of Melos. Staatliche Antikensammlungen, Munich.

embrace and grabbed his opponent around the knees. He then lifted the king up and smashed him down onto his head, killing him instantly. Theseus was thus named as the new king of Eleusis, but still he carried on in his journey to Athens.

Procrustes the Stretcher

As Theseus approached Athens, he passed by Mount Korydallos, the home of Procrustes, yet another son of the promiscuous Poseidon. Procrustes was a smith who had made two iron beds. He never failed to offer travelers lodging for the night, and he always made sure that they only saw a bed that did not fit them. If the guest was too short, Procrustes would stretch them until they were exactly long enough; if they were too tall, he lopped off their legs by the required amount.

Theseus overcame Procrustes and, like the earlier adversaries on his journey to Athens, he gave the mad smith a dose of his own medicine. When Procrustes attempted to tie Theseus to his bed, the young hero leapt up and bound Procrustes to it instead. Seeing that the bed was far too short, Theseus took Procrustes' own axe, and hacked off the murderer's legs before lopping off his head. Deciding not to spend the night on Mount Korydallos, Theseus continued on his way.

Arrival in Athens

When Theseus finally reached Athens, he found that he was no safer there than he had been on the road. His father Aegeus had married for a third time. His new wife was the sorceress Medea, who had come to Athens after murdering her children by Jason when the leader of the Argonauts had abandoned her for another woman. Medea had given Aegeus his long-awaited heir, a boy named Medus, but as the older son Theseus had a strong claim to the throne of Athens.

Theseus did not reveal his identity to Aegeus immediately, preferring to wait and see how things stood in Athens. Aegeus, for his part, offered hospitality to the young stranger, but was suspicious of his intentions.

Medea, though, had no doubts whatsoever. She recognized Theseus right away as the son of Aegeus, and began to worry what his arrival might mean for her own son's future. Hoping to get rid of him, Medea challenged Theseus to capture the Marathonian Bull, expecting that he would be killed in the attempt.

The Marathonian Bull

The Marathonian Bull was a huge and fierce animal that had originally come from Crete. Hercules had subdued the beast as part of his Seventh Labor, and brought it to Athens as a sacrifice to Hera. Hera refused the sacrifice, however, because she hated Hercules for being the illegitimate son of her husband Zeus from his affair with the mortal princess Alcmene. As a result, the bull wandered the plain of Marathon outside Athens, terrorizing the area.

Despite Medea's hopes, Theseus overpowered the bull and brought it back to Athens where it was sacrificed to Zeus. The furious Medea then tried to poison Theseus at a feast. However, the old king Aegeus finally caught on. He recognized the sandals that Theseus wore and the sword he carried. He also recognized the murderous glint in his wife's eye. Just before Theseus took a sip from the poisoned chalice, Aegeus dashed the cup from Theseus' hand. Father and son were reunited, and Medea fled to her father's domain of Colchis on the Black Sea, taking Medus with her.

The Fifty Sons of Pallas

The Sons of Pallas, or Pallantides, were a powerful faction of nobles from Attica, the region that surrounds Athens. They were nephews of Aegeus, and hoped to take control of Athens if he died childless. When Aegeus' son Medus had fled along with his mother, Theseus replaced him as an obstacle to their ambitions.

They attacked Athens soon after Medea fled determined to take the city by force. The Sons of Pallas split their forces into two divisions. One marched on Athens openly to draw the Athenian forces out of the city, while the other lay in ambush planning to attack them in the rear. However, a herald named Leos defected from the Sons of Pallas to Athens and warned Theseus of the plan.

Theseus decided to destroy his enemies piecemeal. First he ambushed the ambushers by attacking their camp at night. Despite the confusion of a night

Theseus capturing the Marathonian Bull in a painting by Charles-Andre van Loo.

raid, Theseus managed to slaughter all of his foes. When daybreak came, he turned his army and marched against his enemy on the plains in front of the city. The Sons of Pallas fought with confidence, expecting the ambushing force to appear at any moment. When it didn't, they lost heart, their forces broke, and the Athenians slaughtered them as they tried to run.

Alternate Versions

There are many sources for Theseus' journey to Athens, and most of them differ from each other in minor details. Plutarch's *Life of Theseus*, long considered the most authoritative source on the hero, does not choose between the different versions. On the contrary, Plutarch takes pains to mention every possible version and variant of the tale, including its source.

The version of the tale told in this chapter is the one most familiar today. For the sake of completeness, though, the main differences between this and the alternate versions are given below.

It is sometimes said that Sinis the Pine Bender challenged passers-by to a pine-bending contest rather than enlisting their aid with his own tree. The number of trees also varies, with victims being either flung to their deaths by a single tree or torn apart between two. Perhaps the most significant alternate version has Theseus simply stabbing Sinis to death instead of administering the more poetic justice of killing him with his own murderous device.

The Crommyonian Sow was said by some to have been spawned by Echidna and Typhon, who are known in Greek myth as the mother and father of monsters. Among their other offspring are the Lernean Hydra, the Chimera, the Sphinx, and Cerberus, the three-headed watchdog of Hades. The Greek writer Strabo claims that the Crommyonian Sow was the mother of the Calydonian Boar, while a few sources state that the Crommyonian Sow was actually the boar itself.

In some accounts the Crommyonian Sow was named Phaia after an old crone who had bred it; others claim that the crone and the sow were the same creature, or that "the Crommyonian Sow" was the hag's nickname.

Plutarch says that writers from Sciron's home town of Megara told a different tale from the Athenians. They maintained that Sciron was a good and just ruler who suppressed lawlessness throughout his realm. According to Plutarch, Sciron was related by marriage to both Cychreus, the king of Salamis, and Aeacus, the king of Aegina; both men were renowned for their virtue, he says, and unlikely to have contracted marriage-alliances with a known malefactor. Plutarch also mentions the Megaran claim that Theseus did not slay Sciron on his journey to Athens but some time later, when he conquered Megara's tributary town of Eleusis.

All sources agree that, like Theseus, Cercyon had divine blood, but there is some disagreement about his actual parentage. His father is variously said to have been Poseidon (making him Theseus' half-brother), Hephaestus (making

him a half-brother to Periphetes the Clubber), or a mortal named Branchus; his mother is said to have been the water-nymph Argiope or a daughter of the hero Amphictyon.

The story of Procrustes the Stretcher is more consistent than the others. His lair at Mount Korydallos was so close to Athens that perhaps only the "official" Athenian version was ever told. However, Plutarch mentions that in earlier versions of the tale, the mad smith did not rack his shorter victims: instead, he pounded their legs with his hammer to stretch them out.

The Growth of Athens

The Classical Greek religion, based on the worship of the Olympian gods, superseded an earlier, earth-based religion in which an earth-goddess took a mortal king as a consort – usually for a fixed number of years – before he was sacrificed and replaced. It is thought that the Eleusinian mysteries were one

Theseus fights Cercyon, Procrustes, Sciron, the Marathonian Bull, Sinis, and the Crommyonian Sow on this fifth-century BC cup from Athens. At the center, he drags the Minotaur's corpse from the Labyrinth. (British Museum)

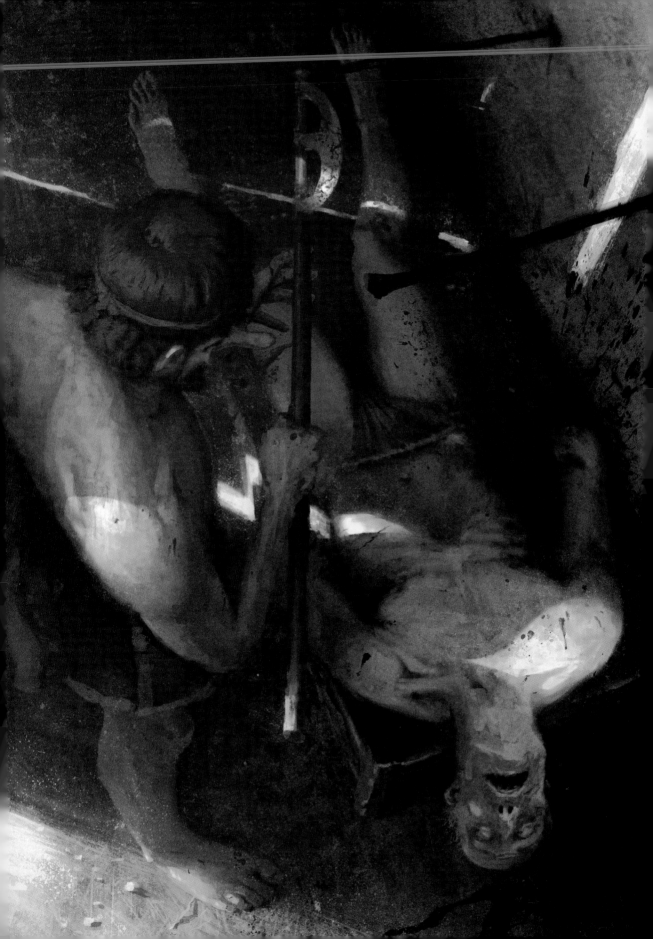

such religion, and there is evidence suggesting that Minoan Crete followed a similar religion.

If it is true that the tales of Theseus reflect the growth and spread of Athenian influence, the most transparent allegory is his encounter with Cercyon, whom he replaces as king of Eleusis. But fainter traces of similar allegories can be seen in his other encounters on the road to Athens. It is perhaps significant, too, that the locations of his six encounters are sometimes referred to as "the six entrances to the Underworld," investing the tales with an air of religious significance.

While the character of Periphetes the Clubber seems one-dimensional, his status as a son of Hephaestus – and the corresponding traits of lameness and having one eye – hint at a divine nature. It could be that this encounter reflects a historical event wherein Athens gained control of Epidaurus and replaced a local cult of an underworld deity with its own religion and culture.

Theseus' dalliance with Perigune might be seen as an allegory for the kind of sacred marriage characteristic of many earth-cults. Identified in the myth as the daughter of the bandit Sinis, she might originally have been an Isthmian princess-priestess through whom the royal succession passed. In this case, the story once again reflects the growth of Athenian dominance over the Isthmus of Corinth – a vital trade and communication route.

The adventure of the Crommyonian Sow is more obscure. The sow may be a local totem or an allegory for another local culture, but it is hard to draw any firm conclusions.

Plutarch claims that Sciron was not a mere robber, but a prince and warlord of the city of Megara. The story of his encounter with Theseus can be viewed as a distorted account of diplomacy and war. Foot-washing is a sign of humility and submission in many cultures. Pope Francis washed the feet of inmates at an Italian juvenile detention center in March 2013 to demonstrate his humility, and the practice has a long history. Seen in this light, Sciron's demand seems like a demand for formal submission, and Theseus' action in throwing him off a cliff could be seen as a robust Athenian response.

Procrustes is said in some sources to be a son of Poseidon like Theseus, which may indicate the replacement of an older cult by a newer, more Athenian-aligned one. However, as with the adventure of the Crommyonian Sow, information on the bandit is too scant to support any further interpretation.

Although it is possible to see the whole of Theseus' journey to Athens as an allegory for the spread of Athenian political and religious dominance around the Isthmus of Corinth, it is difficult to draw any firm conclusions without sufficient supporting historical or archeological evidence. While the interpretation is an attractive one, it remains no more than speculation until it can be tested against hard data.

(OPPOSITE)
Procrustes forced his victims onto an iron bed, racking them if they were too short to fit it exactly and lopping off their feet if they were too tall.

THESEUS AND THE MINOTAUR – THE MYTH

The Birth of the Minotaur

The story of the Minotaur begins when the young king Minos, himself a son of the god Zeus, called to Poseidon for a sign that the throne of Crete was rightfully his. The sea-god responded by sending Minos a great white bull from the sea. Such a display of godly favor ended all other claims to the throne. In thanks, Minos vowed to sacrifice the bull to Poseidon, but the bull was so magnificent that he changed his mind and sacrificed a different bull instead.

Poseidon was enraged by this duplicity and punished Minos by afflicting his queen, Pasiphae, with an unnatural and obsessive lust for the divine bull. Eventually she convinced the inventor Daedalus to create a wooden cow in which she could hide to copulate with the beast. The result of this unnatural union was a boy who was half man, half bull. His parents named him Asterion after Minos' foster-father, but the Greeks called him the Minotaur, "the Bull of Minos."

The birth of the Minotaur created a dilemma for Minos. If he did nothing, the creature would terrorize his kingdom and publicize the shame of his wife's unnatural lust; however, as the offspring of a divine gift, the monstrous child could not be harmed without risking further offense to Poseidon. Minos solved the problem by having Daedalus construct an elaborate maze, the Labyrinth, as a prison and hiding-place for the monster.

So, from a young age, the Minotaur was imprisoned in the Labyrinth. For food, Minos ordered that slaves and prisoners be cast into the maze on a regular basis so the Minotaur could hunt them, kill them, and eat them.

Daedalus presents Pasiphae with his artificial cow in this Roman mosaic from Pompeii.

The Death of Androgeus

Despite the curse of the Minotaur, the rule of Minos brought power and wealth to the island of Crete. He created a great navy, which he used to clear the Mediterranean of pirates and then to subdue many cities on the Greek mainland. In time, Minos had another son, a boy named Androgeus, who was a gifted athlete and warrior. When he was still a young man, Androgeus travelled to Athens at the time when the Marathonian Bull was laying waste to the countryside. According to the Athenians, Androgeus volunteered to fight the Bull, but the monster killed him.

A Minoan ship depicted in a 16th century BC fresco from Akrotiri at the National Archeological Museum of Athens. Minos threatened Athens with war after the death of his son Androgeus. (The Art Archive / Alamy)

Minos refused to believe the Athenians' story, claiming that they had murdered his son out of fear of the power of Crete. In his anger, Minos commanded his army and navy to assault the city of Athens. Although the city

THE MINOAN CIVILIZATION

Cretan civilization flourished between the 27th and 15th centuries BC, making it a contemporary of the 2nd–16th dynasties of Egypt and the earlier phases of the Mycenaean civilization of mainland Greece. Traces of this civilization were uncovered in the early 20th century by British archeologist Sir Arthur Evans, who coined the term "Minoan" after the legendary King Minos.

The Bronze Age began in Crete around 2700 BC. As the Minoan civilization developed, it gave rise to large and complex palace structures like the one Evans excavated at Knossos. Crete became a major power in the eastern Mediterranean, and the Minoans traded with Egypt, Mycenae, and the Canaanite civilization in present-day Israel, Palestine, and Lebanon.

The eruption of the volcanic island of Thera (modern Santorini) between 1625 and 1600 BC devastated the Minoan civilization, but its palaces were rebuilt and became even more impressive until Crete was overrun by the Mycenaean Greeks between 1475 and 1325 BC. Mycenaean culture had been heavily influenced by Crete, and the Mycenaeans continued to rule until around 1200 BC and the start of the Iron Age in the region.

walls kept the Athenians relatively safe, Minos destroyed all of the surrounding farms and villages. He also called upon the power of his mighty father, and Zeus sent a series of devastating earthquakes against the city. Eventually the Athenians had had enough. They sent a group to the Oracle at Delphi to learn how they could end the siege. The Oracle told them that they must agree to any demands that Minos made.

The Athenians surrendered to Minos. In retaliation for the death of his son, Minos demanded that every nine years the Athenians should send seven young men and seven young women to be sacrificed as tribute in the Labyrinth of the Minotaur.

The Tribute

Soon after Theseus arrived in Athens, the tribute became due for the third time. All of the maidens and young men of Athens were called together, and they drew lots to see who would be sent. Since Theseus was not actually from Athens, he was exempt from the draw, but when he saw the crying mothers, he volunteered to join the tribute. Aegeus tried to talk his son out of it, but Theseus had made up his mind.

Theseus had no intention of quietly surrendering to the Minotaur, however. Instead, he began to concoct a plan. After all of the lots had been drawn, he found two strong and brave young men, who had slightly effeminate faces, and convinced them to take the places of two of the young maidens. He instructed them to dress like the girls, to bath with sweet oils so they would smell like them, and to study the movements of the other girls so they could imitate them.

When the time came to sail to Crete, Theseus led the 13 other members of the tribute aboard a black-sailed ship. Before they cast off, Aegeus came to see his son one last time. He gave to Theseus a set of white sails and made him promise, if he should manage to somehow escape the Minotaur, he would hoist the white sails on his return voyage. That way, Aegeus would know as soon as possible that his son was still alive.

The Challenge of Minos

When the ship arrived in Crete, King Minos and several of his household came down from the palace to view the tribute. As Minos watched the young maidens come ashore, he was immediately struck by the beauty of a girl named Periboea. He seized hold of the girl and would have dragged her away right then to satisfy his lust, if Theseus had not stepped forward to challenge him. Theseus said he was the son of Poseidon, and that it was his duty to protect innocent maidens.

Minos laughed. Then he took a gold ring off his finger and cast it into the ocean. He commanded Theseus to prove that the sea-god was his father, by swimming into the ocean and recovering the ring. Without pause, Theseus dove into the water. Beneath the waves, a friendly school of dolphins guided Theseus down to the palace of the Nereids. There Theseus met Thetis, queen of the Nereids. When Theseus told the queen his story, she commanded her people to go out and find the golden ring. Once they had found it and given it to Theseus, Thetis also gave the young hero her own gold crown as a gift for his courage.

Thus, when Theseus emerged from the ocean to the astonished stares of the Creteans, he not only held Minos' golden ring, but also wore a beautiful crown of gold. Theseus appeared so handsome and kingly that Ariadne, the daughter of Minos, immediately fell in love with him. Meanwhile, furious at having been shown up, Minos relinquished Periboea, but commanded that Theseus be the first of the tribute thrown into the Labyrinth.

Into the Labyrinth

That night, Ariadne came to Theseus in secret. She promised that she would help Theseus to kill the Minotaur and escape the Labyrinth if he would marry her and take her back to Athens. Theseus readily agreed.

The next morning, the soldiers of Crete came and took Theseus to the entrance to the Labyrinth. With nothing but his clothes, the young hero was shoved through the opening and sealed inside. The only light came from a few small windows high above. However, a few minutes later, Ariadne's face appeared

Ariadne and Theseus with his ball of twine at the entrance to the Labyrinth by Jean-Baptiste Regnault. (The Art Gallery Collection / Alamy)

at one of the windows. Through the small opening, she dropped Theseus' sword and a ball of twine. Then she wished him good luck and was gone.

Theseus picked up the ball of twine and tied one end to the entrance to the Labyrinth. Then he took his sword and set off down the twisting passages, trailing the twine behind him. For several hours, Theseus crept through the dark, winding maze. A horrible animal stench filled the air, and broken bones lay scattered across the ground. At times, he heard distant, scraping sounds, like hoofs or horns on rock.

Eventually, Theseus reached the center of the Labyrinth, a large gloomy chamber supported by short columns and filled with the torn and broken bodies of the dead. The mixed stink of

This Roman mosaic from Austria shows Theseus slaying the Minotaur. His black-sailed ship can be seen at the top. Kunsthistorisches Museum, Vienna.

death and manure nearly caused the hero to retch, but he was just able to keep his stomach under control. Then he saw the Minotaur. The hideous beast sat amongst a pile of bodies, tearing semi-rotten flesh from a long bone.

As Theseus stepped into the chamber, it turned to glare at him with one of its small, dark eyes. Then it leaned back its gore-covered head and let out a loud, echoing snort. Theseus gripped his sword tightly as the monster pushed its vast bulk up onto its thick, bull legs. It turned to face him, lowering its long, curved horns so they pointed directly at him. The Minotaur scraped one hoofed foot against the rocky ground, and then it charged.

Theseus waited until the last moment and then leapt to one side, swinging his sword as the beast swept past. The blade clanged off the Minotaur's horn, the sound echoing all around the chamber. The beast skidded to a halt, turned, and charged again. Again, Theseus stepped aside, driving his sword down at the monster's side. Although the stroke was accurate, the point could not penetrate the monster's thick hide.

For a moment the two opponents stopped, both panting from their exertions. Then, with a mighty bellow, the Minotaur charged again. This time, just as the deadly horns bore down on Theseus, he leapt up and over the Minotaur, grabbing one of the horns with his free hand. As Theseus landed, he yanked the Minotaur backwards by its horn, pulling up its head and exposing its throat. Theseus took his father's sword and slashed it across the monster's throat. The Minotaur gave a gurgling cry, then slumped to the ground, dead.

DAEDALUS AND ICARUS

Daedalus was an inventor and artificer of legendary skill. His name means "cunning worker" in ancient Greek.

It is unclear how Daedalus came to be employed by Minos. Some sources state that he created a wide dancing-ground for Minos' daughter Ariadne, which may or may not be the Labyrinth itself.

In order to keep the layout of the Labyrinth secret, Minos locked Daedalus in a tower along with his son and apprentice Icarus. Daedalus contrived to escape by fabricating two pairs of feathered wings. Icarus was killed when he ignored his father's advice and flew too close to the sun, melting the wax that held the feathers onto his wings. Daedalus flew on, eventually reaching Sicily where he took refuge with King Cocalus of Kamikos. Daedalus built a temple to Apollo in thanks for his successful escape, leaving his wings there as an offering.

Minos searched for Daedalus, traveling from city to city in disguise. At each city, he challenged those he met to run a string all the way through a spiral seashell. When Minos reached Sicily, Daedalus gave himself away by succeeding at the task; he tied a string to an ant, which he lured through the spirals of the shell by placing a drop of honey at the far end.

Minos demanded that Cocalus hand Daedalus over, but Cocalus persuaded him to take a bath first. Cocalus' daughters (or in some versions, Daedalus himself) killed Minos in the bath by pouring boiling water over him.

The Athenians claimed that Daedalus was a native of their city, and this is reflected in a tale from his later life. Having escaped Minos and returned to Athens, Daedalus took his sister's son Perdix as an apprentice to replace the fallen Icarus. As Perdix began to surpass him in skill and cunning, the jealous Daedalus caused the boy to fall to his death from the Acropolis, then left Athens to escape the rage of the boy's grieving mother.

The Escape from Crete

In the middle of the night, while Theseus was slowly making his way back out of the Labyrinth, the two young men that Theseus had hidden amongst the maidens cast off their disguises. They surprised their guards, killed them, and then set all of the rest of the tribute free.

They made their way quietly to the entrance of the Labyrinth, where they met Ariadne and her sister Phaedra, who had also decided to run away with the Athenians. Ariadne opened the door of the great maze, and a few minutes later, guided by the twine he had laid as he went in, Theseus appeared, covered in the gore and blood of the Minotaur.

Together, the small group stole its way down to the harbor and boarded the ship that had brought them to Crete. Before they cast off, Theseus went out and stove in the hulls of the Cretan warships to prevent any pursuit. Then the ship, carrying Theseus, Ariadne, Phaedra, and all of the tribute, slipped away into the night.

The Return to Athens

A few days after escaping Crete, Theseus' ship stopped at the island of Naxos. While sleeping onshore, Theseus had a dream that the god Dionysus appeared and demanded that he leave Ariadne behind so that the god could marry her. When Theseus awoke, he saw a dark fleet bearing down upon the island.

(OPPOSITE)
The Cretan princess Ariadne fell in love with Theseus and gave him a ball of twine to help him find his way out of the Labyrinth.

Convinced that the fleet belonged to Dionysus, Theseus ordered everyone back aboard the ship, and cast off. Setting all sails, they escaped the dark fleet, but it wasn't until the next morning that anyone realized that Ariadne had been left behind. Convinced that the whole affair had been arranged by Dionysus, Theseus sailed on. As it turned out, Dionysus did marry Ariadne, and she would eventually bear him many children, but not before she cursed Theseus for abandoning her.

Ariadne's curse would not take long to take effect. As Theseus sailed home, he was still troubled by the dark fleet and breaking his promise to marry Ariadne. So lost was he in these gloomy thoughts that he forgot all about the white sails that his father had given to him to announce his success. As the ship came within sight of Athens, it still carried the black sails. Theseus' father, Aegeus, went up to the top of the Acropolis to see the ship coming in. When he saw the black sails, his heart broke, for he believed his son to be dead. Lost in despair, Aegeus cast himself off the Acropolis and plunged to his death.

Although Theseus arrived back in Athens having defeated the Minotaur and rescued the tribute, it proved a somber homecoming. Still, as the king's son, Theseus was soon afterwards crowned king.

MINOS, THE LABYRINTH, AND THE MINOTAUR – THE HISTORY

The Minotaur was a monstrous creature that was half bull and half human. It is generally depicted as a muscular human with the horned head of a bull; a few more modern depictions also give it bovine legs, similar to the goat legs of a satyr. Theseus' victory against the Minotaur remains his greatest and best-known accomplishment.

King Minos

King Minos of Crete was the son of Zeus and the Phoenician princess Europa, who gave her name to the continent of Europe. He appears in various other legends, and seems to have ruled for a very long time. Plutarch and a few other ancient writers explain this by suggesting that Crete had a succession of rulers named Minos. Some modern scholars believe that "Minos" is derived from the Cretan word for "king," *mi-nu* or *mwi-nu*, making it a title rather than a personal name.

Athenian legends, including the story of Theseus, depict Minos as a cruel tyrant, but his character is very different in tales from Crete and elsewhere. Non-Athenian sources depict Minos as a great and wise ruler, trained in law and statecraft by Zeus himself, who was made one of the three judges of the Underworld after his death.

There is some evidence that Minos was the title given to a king-consort who ruled alongside an earth-goddess (perhaps embodied by a priestess-queen) and was sacrificed and replaced like the year-kings of the Eleusinian Mysteries. "Minos" may originally have meant "war-chief" rather than "king," and is intriguingly similar to the names of mythical founder-kings from several other early cultures: Menes from Egypt, Mizraim of Egypt in the Book of Genesis, Meon from Phrygia and Lydia, Baal Meon from Canaan, and even Mannus from Germany and Manu from India.

It is said that Minos ruled at Knossos for periods of nine years, at the end of which he went into a cave sacred to Zeus in order to consult with him on

Crete's laws and rulership. This sounds very like a mythologized account of a king-consort who was sacrificed at the end of his appointed term.

If this interpretation of Minos' nature is correct, then the myth of Theseus and the Minotaur could be seen as an allegory for a process by which Athens threw off Minoan-Mycenaean cultural domination in the late Bronze Age and began to assert its own culture and religion. In this case, the earlier parts of Theseus' story can be seen as reflecting Athens' early rise to power in mainland Greece, and the next chapter will present additional evidence that the myth may be an allegory for a war between Athens and Crete.

The Cretan Bull

The bull seems to have been an important symbol in Minoan civilization. Images of bulls are commonplace in Minoan contexts: the black steatite *rhyton* drinking vessel and the famous bull-leaping fresco found at Knossos are just two examples.

The Marathonian Bull is said to have come originally from Crete. According to some myths it was the same bull whose form Zeus took when

BULL-GODS

The bull as a symbol of strength and fertility was fairly widespread throughout the ancient Near East.

In the Canaanite pantheon, the gods Ba'al and El were both associated with the bull, and the Golden Calf in the Book of Exodus may have been an idol of one or both. The Sumerian god Marduk is sometimes called "the bull of Utu" (the sun-god). In Egypt, the sacred Apis bull was associated first with Ptah, a creator-god, and later with Osiris; sacred bulls were kept in the temple at Memphis, and mummified after their deaths.

Bull symbolism goes back into the prehistory of the region. At the prehistoric city of Katal Huyuk in Anatolia, the horned skulls of bulls were set into walls and pillars and covered in plaster to give them a lifelike appearance; one chamber, known as the Bull Shrine, featured multiple skulls of various sizes as well as wall-paintings of bulls.

It has been suggested that the bull-gods of the ancient Near East were all descended from a single, long-forgotten fertility cult that was overcome and absorbed by the various regional polytheistic religions at some time in the Neolithic period. If that is the case,

the Minotaur might be interpreted as a remnant of just such a religion that existed on Crete in prehistoric times.

Ancient Greek eye-cup depicting the Minotaur from c. 515 BC. (Heritage Image Partnership Ltd / Alamy)

he seduced the princess Europa. According to others, it was the unnatural father of the Minotaur, making it the same bull that Poseidon sent in answer to Minos' prayer. Hercules brought the bull to Greece as his Seventh Labor, but it ran wild on the Plain of Marathon, spreading fear and destruction until it was finally captured by Theseus.

Given the importance of the bull as a Minoan symbol (and as a symbol of wealth in many early societies), and the fact that much of Minoan Crete's wealth came from maritime trade with Egypt, Greece, and the Middle East, it is possible to see the bull from the sea as a metaphor for Crete's prosperity, and its association with Poseidon as a Greek adaptation of some earlier religious association with a Minoan sea-god.

It may also be significant that in the Greek religion Poseidon was the god of earthquakes as well as of the sea. The Minoan palaces of Crete show signs of several natural disasters, including the devastating eruption of Thera around 1600 BC. Little is known of the Minoan religion, partly due to the Greek habit of equating the gods of other cultures with the "true" gods of their own religion when writing about them, but the divine title "Earthshaker" appears to refer to a bull-god. It is likely that Greek writers are referring to this Minoan deity when they talk about Poseidon and bulls in a Cretan context; in purely Greek myths Poseidon is associated with horses rather than cattle.

Given the comparative dearth of written records from the Minoans themselves, it is only possible to speculate on the significance of the Cretan bull. It might be a symbol of kingship, or of the strength of Minoan culture. It might represent a deity to whom the Minoans believed they owed their prosperity, or one they felt obliged to propitiate with rituals and sacrifices in order to avert earthquakes and volcanic eruptions. Whatever the details may have been, though, it seems certain that the image of the Minotaur is somehow linked to Minoan bull symbolism, and that the Minotaur is more than simply another monster born from a divine curse.

The Labyrinth

In the Theseus myth the Labyrinth was a vast and complex maze, constructed by Daedalus on Minos' orders with the specific purpose of housing the Minotaur. It was so complex that even its own creator was barely able to find his way out once he had finished it, and its name has since become a synonym for a large and elaborate maze. However, some sources explain the Labyrinth differently.

The House of the Axe

The double axe, called *labrys* in Greek, was a potent symbol in the Minoan civilization. Symbolic double axes in bronze and gold have been found in Minoan, Greek, and Thracian contexts dating from the Middle Bronze Age onward, and similar symbols have been found carved into the walls of several Minoan palaces and at earlier urban settlements including Katal Huyuk (also spelled Çatal Hüyük) in Anatolia. Even outside Crete, these images are sometimes accompanied by bull imagery.

Double-axe symbols decorate this clay vessel from eastern Crete. Archeological Museum, Heraklion. (Wolfgang Sauber)

A Linear B inscription tablet found in the palace of Knossos bears a dedication that can be interpreted as referring to "the Lady of the Labyrinth" or "the mistress of the double axe." In either case this person seems to be a goddess of the palace. Based on her mythological role as guardian of the Labyrinth, some scholars have suggested that Ariadne was a priestess – or even a mortal personification – of this deity, and that the double axe was her symbol.

Archeological excavations by Sir Arthur Evans in the early 20th century uncovered the palace at Knossos. Compared to Greek cities of the time it was a very large and complex structure, and it is easy to believe the theory that the mythical labyrinth arose from the impression that this palace made on early Greek visitors with its many rooms and passages.

Ariadne's Dancing-Ground

Another theory suggests that the Labyrinth was not the palace itself, but a dancing-ground in the form of a maze that stood somewhere outside it. Ritual dances were held there to honor the goddess of the double axe. Once again, Ariadne might have been a priestess of the double-axe cult, an embodiment of its goddess, or both. Some classicists, including the British author Robert Graves, have suggested that the name "Ariadne" may be a priestly title derived from *Adnon*, a Cretan-Greek word that according to the fifth-century scholar Hesychius of Alexandria meant "absolutely pure."

Like the Minotaur's Labyrinth, the creation of this dancing-ground is credited to Daedalus. Combining the two stories, the image of the Minotaur at the center of the Labyrinth could be seen as

MINOS THE JUDGE

Although the myth of Theseus continued to be retold in Roman and later times, Minos' role as an Underworld judge assumed greater prominence than his links with Crete and the Minotaur. By contrast with his Cretan image as a wise and just ruler, the Minos of the Underworld is a stern and intimidating judge who decides the fate of each deceased soul.

In Book VI of Virgil's *Aeneid*, Aeneas encounters Minos when he descends into the Underworld to meet his father's shade and receive a prophetic vision of the future glory of Rome. Minos is seen only briefly, sitting beside a great urn filled with colored balls which he uses to assign souls to heavenly Elysium or hellish Tartarus.

Minos is also seen in the Second Circle of Dante's *Inferno* as Virgil guides Dante through the Underworld. Once again he examines newly arrived souls and assigns them to the various circles of Hell according to the nature of their sins. He pauses to warn Dante that he should not enter lightly, but Virgil rebukes him, saying that Dante's visit is foreordained. Minos is described as a grim and fearsome judge with a snarling face and a tail that he wraps around his body.

Minos also appears in Michelangelo's fresco *The Last Judgment* in the Sistine Chapel. He stands at the lower right of the picture, supervising the souls of the damned as they are brought off Charon's boat. As in Dante's poem, he has a snake-like tail wrapped around his body.

Minos is shown judging the dead in this 19th-century engraving by Gustav Doré for Dante's *Inferno*.

part of a fertility ritual in which one or more celebrants representing the goddess danced into the maze to achieve union with a male divine figure represented by the bull-headed man. However, there is insufficient documentary evidence at this time to support any speculations about Minoan religious rituals.

Turf-cut labyrinths have been known in Europe since the Middle Ages and may well be survivors of an earlier tradition. In recent years many have been restored, and maze dances have become a part of some New Age and Wiccan traditions. Labyrinth patterns can also be found on the floors of some European cathedrals, notably those of Chartres, Reims, and Amiens in northern France.

Some local traditions interpret walking a labyrinth – especially one in a cathedral – as making an allegorical journey to the spiritual Jerusalem, the kingdom of God, but there is plenty of evidence that maze-walking traditions predate Christianity across most of Europe, and it is possible that these cathedral labyrinths were Christian adaptations of pagan traditions like the maypole and the Christmas tree.

Finding the Labyrinth

In October 2009, British newspapers reported on an expedition led by Oxford University geographer Nicholas Howarth. Skeptical of Evans' claim that the mythical Labyrinth was based on the palace of Knossos, Howarth and his team explored two underground complexes in Crete hoping to discover evidence to link one of them to the Labyrinth.

The first site, Skotino Cave, is about 10 miles east of Heraklion and a similar distance east-northeast of the palace. Excavations in the 1960s found evidence that the cave had been used as a ritual site from the Minoan period into the Classical Greek and Roman eras. Howarth's expedition concluded that the complex was natural, whereas the Labyrinth of myth was always described as artificially constructed.

Howarth's second site was a tunnel complex at Gortyn, some 30 miles south of Knossos. The tunnels are known locally as the Labyrinthos Caves, and have been associated with the myth of the Labyrinth since at least the 12th century. Interest in them waned after Evans' discovery of the palace of Knossos. Howarth's expedition confirmed that the complex was at least partly artificial, with passages and chambers that had been widened and enlarged in the past. However, nothing was found that could firmly link the site to the myth of the Labyrinth.

Despite the efforts of Howarth and others, it seems unlikely that the Labyrinth of myth will ever be linked unequivocally to a specific location on the island of Crete.

Mazes and Monsters

The myth of Theseus and the Minotaur is one of the oldest surviving examples

THE BULL DANCE

One of the most famous images of the Minoan civilization comes from a fresco found in the palace of Knossos, which shows three athletes with a charging bull. One stands in front, grasping the animal's horns. The second is pictured in mid-somersault with his hands touching the bull's back. The third stands behind the bull with his arms raised, either just landing after his own somersault or preparing to catch the jumper.

This is not the only bull-leaping image to have come from Crete. An ivory figurine of an athlete apparently in flight, also from Knossos, has been interpreted as the only surviving part of a bull-leaping scene. More complete is a small bronze sculpture found at Rethymnon to the west of Knossos and currently in the British Museum in London.

Although the true meaning of these images is still debated, many scholars have suggested that bull-leaping was part of a ritual connected with Minoan bull-worship. It is quite easy to see how the complex layout of the Knossos palace and the sport or ritual of bull-leaping might have become mythologized into a maze-like trap containing a bull-headed monster.

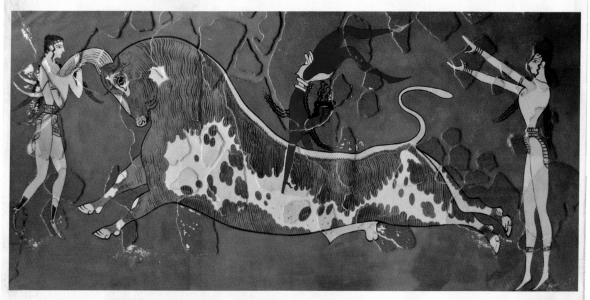

The famous bull-leaping fresco from the palace at Knossos. Was this sport or ritual the origin of the Minotaur myth? (David South / Alamy)

of a tale where a hero confronts a monster in an elaborate building complex. Its role in the myth makes the Labyrinth an ancestor of Tolkien's Mines of Moria, the monster lairs of *Dungeons & Dragons* and other fantasy roleplaying games, and the complex levels of video games like the *Doom* series.

The truth behind the myth of the Labyrinth is open to debate, but it is interesting to note that mazes appear in the mythology and folklore of many parts of the world. Like the Labyrinth, they are most often intended to trap evil spirits, keeping them imprisoned and harmless. This is in contrast to the role of dungeons in modern fantasy, which are usually the lairs of dangerous creatures that must be defeated to ensure the safety of the community.

Linear A and Linear B

The Minoan civilization used three separate writing systems. Linear B was used throughout the Minoan-Mycenaean cultural area and succeeded an earlier, still undeciphered script known as Linear A. Also undeciphered is an even earlier script, which is generally called "Cretan hieroglyphs" and is known only from inscriptions on the island of Crete.

Linear B was deciphered in the 1950s, and up to the time of writing almost 6,000 examples of Linear B writing have been found, mostly on clay tablets. They offer many insights into the language of the time, but are usually too short and fragmentary to give a deep picture of the culture itself.

The Labyrinth at Chartres Cathedral, c 1750. In a Christian context the Labyrinth symbolized a pilgrimage toward spiritual redemption.

THESEUS IN CRETE – VARIATIONS, HISTORY, AND INTERPRETATION

The common thread of the Theseus legend tells that Minos demanded a regular tribute of seven youths and seven maidens from Athens, who were delivered every seven years to be devoured by the Minotaur. Theseus went to Crete as one of these victims, and with the help of Minos' daughter Ariadne he slew the Minotaur and found his way out of the Labyrinth. However, there are multiple versions of the tale, and each one is subject to interpretation. This chapter sets out the different versions of Theseus' adventures in Crete, and discusses their possible meanings.

The Death of the Minotaur

Theseus' best-known exploit is recounted very briefly in the surviving accounts of his adventures. All agree that he entered the Labyrinth, slew the monster, and found his way out thanks to the love-struck Ariadne.

Ariadne gave Theseus a ball of twine – a *clew* in Old English, and possibly the origin of the modern word "clue." Theseus ventured into the Labyrinth, unspooling the twine as he went to leave a trail back out. After a struggle, he slew the Minotaur by stabbing it in the neck. The combat itself is always covered in a few words, with almost no details as to how long the fight lasted or how the two fought.

Although the written accounts of the slaying of the Minotaur are scanty, it is a favorite topic in art from Classical times to the present day. Many Greek vase-paintings show Theseus stabbing the Minotaur or dragging its body from the Labyrinth as Ariadne – or sometimes Athena, the patron goddess of Athens – looks on.

Theseus slays the Minotaur in this 19th-century bronze by Antoine-Louis Barye. Walters Art Museum, Baltimore. (The Art Archive / Alamy)

As in the rest of Theseus' adventures, different sources vary in minor details. In some versions, Ariadne gave Theseus verbal directions instead of a ball of twine. Relaying instructions from Daedalus himself, she told Theseus to go forward, never left or right, and down whenever possible.

Accounts of the Minotaur's death also vary. In some versions, Ariadne gave Theseus the sword with which he killed the Minotaur, while in others he strangled the monster with his bare hands.

Ariadne

In the most frequently told version of the story, Theseus took Ariadne and her sister Phaedra with him when he set out from Crete after slaying the Minotaur. He abandoned Ariadne on the island of Naxos, where she became the bride of the wine-god Dionysus and bore him several children. According to some writers, Dionysus appeared to Theseus in a vision shortly after he left Crete,

Bacchus and Ariadne by Jacopo Amigoni, c.1740. After Theseus left her on the island of Naxos, Ariadne married the wine-god Dionysius, known to the Romans as Bacchus.

claiming Ariadne as his bride; if so, this conveniently absolved Theseus of any blame for deserting her. It is said that Dionysus gave Ariadne the constellation Corona Borealis, which lies between the constellations of Hercules and Ursa Major or the Great Bear, as her wedding diadem.

According to some tales, Theseus had two sons by Ariadne, named Staphylus ("grape cluster") and Oenopion ("wine drinker"). Given their names it is easy to believe the other writers who claim that these two were actually sons of Dionysus.

Phaedra became Theseus' wife after he left Naxos. She bore him two sons, Demophon and Acamas. Later, while Theseus was trapped in the Underworld, she fell tragically in love with his son Hippolytus. This story will be told in a later chapter.

Plutarch also mentions a tradition from Naxos that claimed there were two Ariadnes, meaning that the Cretan princess abandoned on Naxos by Theseus was not the same person as the wife of Dionysus.

Yet another version of the tale, credited by Plutarch to the lost Cypriot historian Paeon of Amathus, tells that Theseus left Ariadne on that island and not Delos. Theseus and his companions were driven to Cyprus by a storm on their return journey. Ariadne was pregnant at the time and the violent motion of the ship caused her great distress. Theseus managed to put her ashore before being swept out to sea again, and although the women of Cyprus did everything they could for her, Ariadne died in childbirth before Theseus could return. The grieving Theseus gave money for sacrifices in her honor and set up two cult images, one in silver and one in bronze, in a sacred grove that became known as the grove of Aphrodite-Ariadne.

In the account of Cleidemus cited by Plutarch, Ariadne never left Crete. Instead, she succeeded to the throne of Minos after Theseus slew Prince Deucalion at the gates of the Labyrinth. She and Theseus agreed a peace treaty between Crete and Athens, and Ariadne stayed behind to rule Crete when Theseus sailed away. Other versions of the myth tell that Ariadne hanged herself out of grief when Theseus left, making her a tragic queen like Dido in Book IV of Virgil's *Aeneid*.

The Crane-Dance of Delos

According to Plutarch, Theseus also visited the island of Delos on his way back from Crete. He and his companions made sacrifices and offered up a statue of Aphrodite that Theseus had been given by Ariadne. They also performed a winding, turning dance that was said to represent the windings of the Labyrinth and which became a tradition on the island. Its name was reported by Dicaearchus, a student of Aristotle, as the "crane dance." Plutarch also reports that Theseus also instituted games on Delos – perhaps in honor of Ariadne – and that it was at these games that he started the tradition of awarding a palm to the victor of an athletic contest.

THE SHIP OF THESEUS

Plutarch wrties that the ship on which Theseus returned to Athens was a vessel of 30 oars. The Athenians preserved it as a monument to their great hero, and it could be seen in Athens up to the third century BC – about a thousand years after his famous voyage.

The ship was lovingly maintained all that time. As parts decayed they were removed and carefully replaced with sound timber, and because of this practice the Ship of Theseus gave its name to a philosophical paradox. As Plutarch said, "the ship became an illustration to philosophers of the doctrine of growth and change, as some argued that it remained the same, and others that it did not remain the same." Briefly put, if its parts were constantly being replaced, when did the Ship of Theseus stop being the Ship of Theseus?

Socrates and Plato both explored the paradox of the Ship of Theseus, and so did many later philosophers including Thomas Hobbes and John Locke. A modern version of the paradox is sometimes called "George Washington's (or Abe Lincoln's) Axe," and instead of a ship it considers an axe that has had its head replaced twice and its handle three times since its famous owner last touched it.

Other Traditions

General Taurus

In his *Life of Theseus*, Plutarch cites a Cretan version of the tale passed on by the earlier Greek historian Philochorus. The work of Philochorus survives only in fragments, and the original passage to which Plutarch refers has not been found.

According to Plutarch, the Cretan tradition is far more prosaic than the Athenian myth. The Labyrinth was a grim prison from which escape was impossible. Its governor was a brutal – but mortal – general with the highly suggestive name of Taurus, meaning "bull" in Greek. The Athenian hostages were imprisoned in the Labyrinth and given as slaves to the victors in a regular series of memorial games that Minos held in honor of the murdered Androgeus.

The general's strength and ferocity were such that he was expected to dominate the games, but according to Plutarch "his great influence and his unpopular manners made him disliked," and scandal said that he was too intimate with Pasiphae – an intriguing correspondence with the tale of the Minotaur's conception. Therefore when Theseus offered to challenge Taurus in the games, Minos readily agreed.

Theseus excelled in the games, humiliating Taurus in a wrestling match, and his prowess caused Ariadne to fall in love with him. Minos was delighted at the downfall of his powerful but arrogant general. He immediately freed the Athenian captives and declared a permanent end to the tribute.

It is easy to see how a historical figure with the name – or title – of Taurus might have developed into the mythological Minotaur, "the bull of Minos." Plutarch seems to imply that the accounts of Philochorus and Cleidemus (see below) refer to the same events; if so, then General Taurus would seem to be the same person as Minos' son Deucalion.

Alternatively, Plutarch quotes another lost ancient writer named Demon who reported that General Taurus was killed in a sea battle when Theseus and his companions sailed from Crete, taking Ariadne with them.

Theseus stands over the defeated Minotaur in this 1791 painting by Charles Édouard Chaise. (Peter Horree / Alamy)

Theseus Attacks

In addition to this Cretan tradition, Plutarch mentions an account by the now-lost Greek author Cleidemus, who ignores the story of the tribute and the Minotaur altogether and maintains that Theseus led an Athenian attack on Crete that resulted in Ariadne taking the throne of Minos and ruling Crete in her own right.

According to this account, Daedalus fled to Athens rather than Sicily. Minos pursued him in a fleet of war galleys, violating "a decree passed by all Greeks" banning all ships with a crew of more than five hands. The sole exception to this decree was Jason, who was empowered to cruise at will in the *Argo* and keep the sea free from pirates.

41

Minos' expedition ended in failure. He died when his fleet was driven to Sicily by a storm – a plausible alternative reading of his death by "boiling water" at the hands of King Cocalus of Sicily. Minos' son Deucalion sent "a warlike message" to the Athenians, threatening that unless Daedalus was handed over he would kill all the children whom Minos had taken as hostages. It is not made clear whether these hostages had any connection to the death of Androgeus. Theseus replied with peaceful overtures, playing for time while he secretly built ships at Troezen and elsewhere, "far from any place of resort of strangers."

The fleet's arrival in Crete was a complete surprise, and the Athenians took the harbor before the Cretans knew what was happening. Theseus slew Deucalion and his bodyguard at the gates of the Labyrinth, leaving Ariadne as the heir to Minos' throne. Theseus made peace with her, reclaimed the Athenian hostages, and went home after he and Ariadne had concluded a mutual non-aggression pact between Athens and Crete.

While it is very different from the main body of the Theseus myth, this account has enough elements in common with it to make it possible that the myth grew up as an allegory based on historical events that happened more or less as Cleidemus describes. Theseus has a hidden fleet instead of a hidden weapon. He slew a son of Minos at the gates of the Labyrinth and saved Athenian hostages. He forged friendly relations with Ariadne, which brought an end to the conflict between Athens and Crete. It is also interesting to note how Cleidemus explains the voyage of the *Argo* – the subject of another book in this series – as an ongoing anti-piracy mission rather than a search for a fabled treasure.

KING OF ATHENS

There are no contemporary documents to tell us about Theseus' rule in Athens. Almost everything we know comes from Plutarch's biography; most of the earlier sources he quotes have been lost.

The picture that emerges is of Theseus as a tireless reformer who both expanded Athens' regional influence and also reformed its political institutions. Although Plutarch never says so, it is clear that the Athenians regarded Theseus' reforms as laying the foundations both for their later democracy and for the enormous power and influence that their city would come to wield.

Attica

In the late Bronze Age, Attica was a collection of squabbling city-states. According to tradition, Theseus' distant predecessor Cecrops had organized the region into 12 districts and established common religious and political practices, but they remained independent of each other.

As king of Athens, Theseus set about unifying Attica under Athenian leadership. He decreed that all the inhabitants of Attica should receive Athenian citizenship and instructed the various communities to put aside their previous feuds and regard themselves as a single people. He traveled from settlement to settlement, using his fame and Athens' power to win popular support for his plan, while soothing the concerns of the ruling classes by saying that this new commonwealth would have no king; instead, Theseus would act only as its war-leader and chief magistrate.

As the various communities of Attica agreed to his plan – either wholeheartedly or out of reluctance to flout his growing power – Theseus had their individual public buildings pulled down and replaced them with a centralized senate house and *prytaneum*, or sacred hearth, in Athens on the site of the present-day Acropolis.

Plutarch also tells us that Theseus instituted the Panathenaic Games and festival to help bind together the people of his new Athenian commonwealth. This seems to be a contradiction, because earlier he tells

A statue of Theseus in Syntagma Square, Athens. Theseus is credited with laying the foundations for the city's future greatness. (Nikos Pavlakis / Alamy)

43

how Androgeus came from Crete to take part in those games. However, other historical sources trace the origin of the Panathenaic Games to the reign of the tyrant Peisistratus in 556 BC, long after Theseus lived. Perhaps the Panathenaic Games of Plutarch's time developed out of the older Pan-Athenian Games during the time of Peisistratus, and the story of Theseus was invoked to cloak them in an aura of tradition and historical respectability.

Athens

Despite the vagueness of many details, Plutarch's account makes it clear that Theseus reshaped Athens and laid the foundation for its future political, economic, and military importance in Attica. Theseus' social and political reforms in Athens itself helped develop the city into a fitting capital for his new commonwealth.

He organized the city's population into three classes. The educated *Eupatridae* or nobles provided priests, magistrates, and lawyers. The *Demiurgi* were skilled artisans, and the *Geomori* were farmers. Plutarch is careful to emphasize that Theseus did not set any class above the others, "thinking that the nobles would always excel in dignity, the farmers in usefulness, and the artisans in numbers."

Theseus also created an annual holiday for what he called "resident aliens" on the 16th day of the month of Hekatombaion (late July to early August). As well as celebrating the city's non-Athenian population, this festival must also have encouraged talented and ambitious outsiders to come to the city by smoothing over any potential tensions between them and their native Athenian neighbors. The celebration must also have sent the message to the rest of Attica that while Athens was undoubtedly the capital, those from other parts of Attica would be welcome and valued in the city.

According to Plutarch this holiday was still observed in his own time, although as with the games, it may be that the holiday's origin was attributed to Theseus as a matter of civic pride.

Plutarch also reports that Theseus issued coins bearing the image of a bull, in reference either to his capture of the Marathonian Bull or to his exploits in Crete. Although it cannot be proved, this reference could be taken to imply that Theseus reformed the Athenian currency as well as its social and political organization. What is certain is that this powerful symbol of their leader's achievements must have bolstered civic and regional pride, while reminding potential rivals of Theseus' abilities and achievements.

The Isthmus

The Isthmus of Corinth, which Theseus had crossed on his first journey from Troezen to Athens, became the southern and western frontier of the new Athenian commonwealth. Theseus enlarged Attica by annexing Megara and erected a two-sided pillar in the Isthmus, inscribed on the one side with the words "This is not Peloponnesus, but Ionia," and on the other with "This is Peloponnesus, not Ionia."

Peloponnesus (modern Peloponnese) refers to the part of Greece that lies south of the Isthmus. The later war between Athens and the southern city of Sparta became known as the Peloponnesian War because it was effectively a conflict between the north and south of Greece. *Ionia* is probably synonymous with Attica in this context, since the Attic dialect belongs to the Ionian language group. In other contexts, Ionia is most commonly used to refer to the Greek-speaking settlements of western Anatolia, across the Aegean in modern Turkey.

Theseus is also credited with establishing the Isthmian Games in honor of Poseidon. It has been suggested that he did so to atone for killing Sciron, who like him was a son of the sea-god. Other accounts say that the games commemorated Sinis, perhaps because they took place close to the site of Theseus' encounter with the tree-bending bandit. Whatever their religious significance, these games held near the frontier with Peloponnesus would also have provided a perfect opportunity to demonstrate Athenian power to Attica's southern neighbors.

Delphi

With everything organized in Athens and Attica, Theseus laid his power aside and visited the famous Oracle at Delphi to ask for guidance in formulating a constitution for the Athenian commonwealth. According to Plutarch he received this reply:

> Thou son of Aegeus and of Pittheus' maid,
> My father hath within thy city laid
> The bounds of many cities; weigh not down
> Thy soul with thought; the bladder cannot drown.

Plutarch does not attempt to interpret the Oracle's pronouncement, but the words "weigh not down thy soul with thought" seem to indicate that the gods were satisfied with the new arrangement. "My father hath within thy city laid the bounds of many cities" seems to imply that Athens would prosper under the patronage of the gods – especially Apollo, whose temple was the seat of the famous Oracle, and Zeus, Apollo's father and the supreme ruler of the Olympian gods.

The words "the bladder cannot drown" are also interesting. When Theseus was conceived, his father Aegeus was visiting Troezen for help in interpreting another Delphic oracle, which advised him, "Do not loosen the bulging mouth of the wineskin until you have reached the height of Athens, lest you die of grief." It

The Isthmus of Corinth photographed from NASA's Terra satellite. Theseus placed the southern border of his Athenian commonwealth at this strategic land-bridge between northern and southern Greece.

THE ISTHMIAN GAMES

Although Plutarch credits Theseus with instituting the Isthmian Games, they have a much longer history, which dates back to mythic times.

The Isthmian Games were held every two years, in the years immediately before and after each Olympic Games. They are said to have originated as funeral games for Melicertes, a boy prince of Thebes whose mother Ino threw herself and her son into the sea after being stricken with madness by a vengeful Hera. Ino had raised her nephew Dionysus, who was the illegitimate son of Hera's husband Zeus by Ino's sister Semele.

The soul of Melicertes was transformed into a sea-god named Palaemon, a protector of sailors, while dolphins delivered the body of the dead prince to the shore where it was discovered by Sisyphus, the king of Corinth. Sisyphus arranged Melicertes' burial and held funeral games in his honor, which went on to become the Isthmian Games. Sisyphus would later become famous for his mythological punishment in Tartarus for his continued lying; he was condemned to roll a rock up a hill for eternity, only to see it roll down the other side of the hill each time it reached the top.

While Theseus may not have instituted the Isthmian Games, he certainly did expand them. They went from being a closed and largely religious event to a full-scale athletic competition open to all Greeks, with events that rivaled those of the Olympics. Athenian visitors were guaranteed front-row seats. The games were covered by a truce that allowed athletes to come from all over Greece, even in time of war. The truce held even in 412 BC when Athens and Corinth themselves were at war.

The Isthmian Games lasted into Roman times but were eventually suppressed by the Christian emperor Theodosius I (AD 347–95), who regarded them as a pagan ritual. Because their origins are lost in the mists of antiquity it is hard to say exactly how long the Isthmian Games were held, but it must have been at least 1,500 years.

is striking that it cautions Aegeus to take care of a wineskin, while Theseus is reassured that a bladder will be safe; is it possible that both are metaphors for Athens itself, or for the bloodline or legacy of Aegeus and Theseus?

Leaving Athens

According to Plutarch, not everyone was happy with Theseus' political reforms. Some nobles resented their loss of power, and while Theseus was trapped in the Underworld (see next chapter) one Mnestheus formed them into a single conspiracy. When the warrior brothers Castor and Pollux arrived to take Helen back from Athens (see next chapter) and captured the nearby town of Aphidnae (the modern suburb of Afidnes), the Athenians surrendered in fear and not only returned Helen, but also allowed the brothers to take Theseus' mother Aethra back to Sparta with them.

When Theseus finally returned to Athens after Hercules rescued him from Hades' realm, he found that the people were no longer willing to submit meekly to his rule. After a number of disputes he secretly sent his children away to safety and left Athens to go to the island of Skyros, cursing its people.

Plutarch mentions two opinions why Theseus went to Skyros. One tradition claims he wanted to live in quiet retirement, while the other maintains that he wanted to enlist the help of King Lycomedes of Skyros and retake Athens.

THESEUS' OTHER ADVENTURES

Theseus took part in many adventures aside from his journey to Athens and his defeat of the Minotaur. He struck up a friendship with Pirithous, a prince of the Lapith people of Thessaly, and the two had many adventures together. He accompanied Hercules to the land of the Amazons. He took part in the epic hunt for the Calydonian Boar along with many other Greek heroes. Some writers even claim that he sailed with Jason and the Argonauts. Along the way, he seems to have fathered a large number of children with various prominent women, some of whom he married.

Theseus and Pirithous by José Daniel Cabrera Peña

The chronology of these adventures is unclear. Partly this is because, as with all the stories of Theseus, there are so many different and contradictory versions of the stories. Partly, too, it is because the writers who told of his "guest appearances" in the tales of other heroes did not worry about creating a coherent shared timeline.

Details in some accounts imply that more than one of these adventures took place before Theseus' encounter with the Minotaur, but in Plutarch and most of the other sources they are told after that story, bracketing the hero's most famous victory with lesser tales. This book takes the same approach. The various stories in this chapter are told as the sources give them, with little attempt to address these chronological problems.

Theseus and Pirithous

Pirithous was a prince of the Lapiths, one of several peoples who lived in Thessaly to the north of Attica. A grandson of Zeus, he was a hero in his own right, although not as prominent as Theseus.

"NOT WITHOUT THESEUS"

Plutarch quotes an Athenian proverb, "not without Theseus." To the Athenians, no historical or mythological event of any significance could possibly have taken place without their great hero. To use the language of comic books, he was "retconned" into the stories of almost every other great hero in Greek mythology.

Hearing of Theseus' renown, Pirithous decided to put the hero of Athens to the test. He stole Theseus' cattle from the plain of Marathon to provoke him into a chase, and the two fought each other to a standstill. Each was so impressed with the other's fighting prowess that they took an oath of friendship on the spot, and Pirithous accompanied Theseus on a number of his later adventures.

The Lapiths and the Centaurs

The best-known story about Theseus and Pirithous takes place at the latter's wedding to a lady named Hippodamia. Little is known of her. She is said to be the daughter of one Atrax, who was himself the son of the Thessalian river-god Peneus. There was a city in Thessaly named Atrax or Atracia, which stood on the banks of the river Peneus, so it is possible that Hippodamia was a princess of this city and the marriage was to be part of a diplomatic arrangement.

The neighboring Centaurs, a wild folk with human torsos on the bodies of horses, got drunk at the wedding feast and tried to carry off the bride and several other Lapith women. In the ensuing battle Theseus killed Eurytus, the fiercest of the Centaurs.

As human-animal hybrids, the Centaurs are sometime seen as symbols of the lower aspects of human nature; the Minotaur has been interpreted in the same light. In this interpretation, the story of the wedding is an allegory of the struggle

Theseus and Centaur by Antonio Canova. Kunsthistorisches Museum, Vienna. (imageBROKER / Alamy)

between wholly-human civilization and half-wild barbarism. Other writers, including the novelist Mary Renault, have interpreted the centaurs as a horse culture similar to those of the Eurasian steppes, whose symbol and totem may have been a horse.

The battle of the Lapiths and the Centaurs, called the *Centauromachy* in Classical Greek, was a favorite subject for artists from Classical times up to the Renaissance.

Eurytus the Centaur by José Daniel Cabrera Peña

Helen and Persephone

Since Theseus was a son of Poseidon and Pirithous was a grandson of Zeus, the two heroes decided that they would each take a daughter of Zeus as a bride. Theseus chose the Spartan princess Helen, the sister of Castor and Pollux: this was before she had caught the eye of the Trojan prince Paris, leading him to carry her away to Troy and start the Trojan War. The two promptly kidnapped the young princess and left her either in Athens with Theseus' his mother Aethra or at nearby Aphidnae with a trusted friend named Aphidnus.

Pirithous, meanwhile, had set his sights on Persephone, the wife of Hades. The two heroes went to the Underworld, where Hades pretended to receive them hospitably. However, as soon as they sat down to a welcome feast they found themselves trapped by great snakes that coiled around their feet. In another version, the chairs on which the two sat were enchanted to cause forgetfulness and they sat there for an unspecified length of time. According to a third version, Theseus paused to rest near the hellish abyss of Tartarus and

HOMOEROTIC SUBTEXT

Some scholars have seen the close relationship between Theseus and Pirithous as being more than an average male friendship. Homosexuality was more generally accepted in Classical Greek society than in many later ages, and it has been suggested that the two heroes were lovers as well as friends. While both of them had relations with numerous women, many of these liaisons seemed to be nothing more than sexual conquests or political arrangements, and all were short-lived compared to the friendship between the two heroes.

In his account of the hunt for the Calydonian Boar,

Ovid has Theseus address Pirithous as "dearer far than is myself" and "half of my soul." Later Attic comedies told a ribald version of the Underworld adventure in which Theseus left his buttocks stuck to the rock when Hercules pulled him free, and gave Theseus the suggestive name *hypolispos* – "he whose hindquarters are rubbed smooth."

As with many other male relationships in Classical Greek history and myth, there has been a great deal of discussion about a possible homoerotic subtext in the tales of Theseus and Pirithous, but nothing has been found that has decided the question one way or the other.

PREVIOUS PAGE
At the wedding feast of
Theseus' friend Pirithous,
drunken centaurs tried to
carry off the bride and other
Lapith women.

found himself unable to rise from the rock on which he had sat down; the two heroes were instantly surrounded by the Furies, three vicious winged demons, who dragged Pirithous away while Theseus watched helplessly.

Months later, Hercules came to the Underworld on his Twelfth Labor, to capture Hades' three-headed watchdog Cerberus. He found Theseus and freed him from his seat. Persephone forgave Theseus for his part in the attempt to kidnap her, but Pirithous was not so lucky. The whole Underworld trembled when Theseus tried to rescue his friend and the hero of Athens was forced to return to the upper world alone. Plutarch tells a slightly different version, saying that Pirithous was killed by Cerberus.

Theseus returned to Athens to find things had changed in his absence. Spartan forces led by Helen's brothers Castor and Pollux had taken the princess back, and Theseus' mother Aethra was now a captive in Sparta.

In most versions of this tale Helen is said to be a child: various sources give her age as seven or ten. The early (seventh-century BC) Greek poet Stesichorus implies that she was older by making her and Theseus the parents of Iphigenia, who appears in Homer's *Iliad* as a human sacrifice offered so that the Greek fleet could set sail for Troy. Homer follows the accounts of most other writers by making Iphigenia the daughter of Menelaus' brother Agamemnon, the king of Mycenae.

The Furies by José Daniel
Cabrera Peña

THE AMAZONS

In Greek myth, the Amazons were a race of female warriors who lived on the southeastern coast of the Black Sea in Pontus, a part of modern Turkey.

According to some ancient sources, the Amazons did not allow men to reside in their territory. Once a year they visited a neighboring tribe to prevent their race from dying out. Male children were either killed or returned to their fathers, and girls were raised in the Amazon culture.

Recent archeological discoveries in Russia and Ukraine have revealed that the Scythian-Sarmatian culture of the area had a high proportion of female warriors: up to 25 percent of the warrior burials excavated in the region belong to women. The Sarmatians flourished from the fifth century BC to the fourth century AD, and from the reports of Greek and Roman writers they seem to have been a nomadic culture like many on the Eurasian steppes.

Theseus and the Amazons

At some time before he went to Crete, Theseus went to the land of the Amazons. The Amazons welcomed Theseus and sent one of their number – a daughter of the war-god Ares named Antiope – aboard Theseus' ship with gifts. Theseus set sail once she was aboard, and she became his wife, bearing him a son whom they named Hippolytus.

As with the other Theseus myths, there are many variations on this tale. Some say that Theseus was accompanying Hercules, either on his Ninth Labor to recover the magical girdle of the Amazon queen Hippolyta or on some other expedition. Some say that Antiope was captured in battle and given to Theseus in recognition of his valor. Another tale tells that Theseus settled with Antiope for some time in her own land, leaving only when one of his companions committed suicide out of unrequited love for his leader's wife. One tells that Antiope had fallen in love with Theseus and abandoned her people willingly.

Soon afterward the Amazons attacked Athens, intent on recovering both Antiope and Hippolyta's girdle. Plutarch dismisses the suggestion that another motive was to avenge Antiope's honor after Theseus abandoned her for Phaedra.

Peace was concluded after a hard-fought battle in which Antiope was killed. Plutarch states that she was slain by an Amazon javelin while fighting at Theseus' side, while other sources report that she was slain by Theseus while fighting with her Amazon sisters, despite the fact that she was pregnant with Theseus son, Htippolytus, who would play a crucial part in his father's later life.

Phaedra and Hippolytus

The story of Phaedra and Hippolytus is the great tragedy of Theseus' later life, and has been adapted for the stage by the Greek tragedian Euripides, the Roman writer Seneca, and the 17th-century French playwright Racine.

Amphora depicting the abduction of Antiope by Theseus and Pirithous, c. 500-490 BC. (Bridgeman Art Library)

Phaedra, it will be remembered, was the sister of Ariadne, and Theseus brought her to Athens with him after abandoning Ariadne on Naxos. The fact that Hippolytus was grown at this time places Theseus' adventures among the Amazons before his voyage to Crete.

Hippolytus was a devout follower of Artemis, the goddess of hunting, and like many of her followers he had sworn a vow of chastity. This offended Aphrodite, the goddess of love, and she caused Phaedra to fall in love with her stepson.

Tormented by love, Phaedra became ill. Finally she confided the cause of her sickness to a nurse, who told Hippolytus that Phaedra loved him. Afraid of being caught breaking the confidence of her mistress, the nurse swore Hippolytus to secrecy.

After Phaedra died – either by starving herself or through a more active suicide – Theseus found a note on her body that accused Hippolytus of raping her. Enraged, Theseus confronted his son, who could not defend himself without breaking his vow of secrecy to the nurse. Theseus cursed his son, invoking his father Poseidon to deal out punishment.

Hippolytus left for a life of exile. As he drove his chariot away from Athens, Poseidon sent a sea monster (or a wild bull, in some versions), which terrified Hippolytus' horses and caused his chariot to crash. Hippolytus was dragged to his death, tangled in the reins.

Phaedra and Hippolytus by Baron Pierre Narcisse Guerin from 1802. (Peter Horree / Alamy)

According to Euripides and Seneca, Artemis herself appeared to Theseus after his son's death and told him the truth of the affair. Some writers believed that his grief is what compelled Theseus to leave Athens and retire to the palace of King Lycomedes of Skyros, where he met his death.

Theseus in Other Myths

Theseus' encounters with Hercules and Helen of Troy have already been described, but he also appears in many other Greek myths, usually in a minor role.

Jason and the Argonauts

Various sources for the voyage of the *Argo* list Theseus as among the Argonauts, although no particular deeds are ascribed to him. However, it is hard to believe that Theseus was one of Jason's companions on that heroic voyage.

According to the myth of the Argonauts, Jason met Medea on the voyage and married her some time later. It was not until many years later that Medea married King Aegeus of Athens, where the young Theseus first encountered her.

Adventures with Hercules

Theseus crossed paths with Hercules on four occasions, and though the problems of chronology are not as severe as they are in the claims that he was an Argonaut, they are still troubling.

The pair's first encounter took place when Theseus was a child, at some time after Hercules had completed his First Labor, the slaying of the Nemean Lion.

Hercules' Seventh Labor was to capture the Cretan Bull, which was the father of the Minotaur. Allowing time for Pasiphae to fall in love with the bull and give birth to the Minotaur, this must have been at least 15 years before Theseus went to Crete; he was part of the third Athenian tribute, which was levied every seven (or nine) years.

Theseus' adventures among the Amazons may or may not have taken place at the same time as Hercules' Ninth Labor. It could be that there were originally two separate stories that were combined by later writers.

Finally, Hercules was engaged in his Twelfth Labor when he rescued Theseus from the Underworld.

Almost all sources agree that Hercules served Eurystheus, who gave him the Twelve Labors to perform, for ten years. Plutarch, on the other hand, quotes an earlier source that states that Theseus was 50 years old when he carried off Helen, at the start of the adventure that ended with Hercules rescuing him from the Underworld. Given that Theseus was

Hercules by José Daniel Cabrera Peña

(OPPOSITE)
When he tried to help
Pirithous kidnap Hades' bride
Persephone, Theseus was
trapped in the Underworld
before Hercules came to
rescue him.

a child when Hercules completed his First Labor, this is impossible. Time is usually imprecise in Greek myths, of course, but this mismatch suggests that the story of the Twelve Labors existed first and Hercules' various appearances in the life of Theseus were added later.

The Calydonian Boar

Calydon was a city in the region of Aetolia in western Greece. Its king, Oenus ("wine-man") offended the goddess Artemis by forgetting to include her in a series of annual sacrifices he made to the gods, and she sent a great and terrible boar to ravage the surrounding countryside. In response to the king's call for help, a veritable super-team of Greek heroes assembled to hunt the beast down.

Ravaging boars appear quite frequently in Greek myth. We have already seen how Theseus overcame the Crommyonian Sow, and the Greek geographer Strabo went so far as to claim that the Calydonian Boar was her offspring. Hercules vanquished the Erymanthian Boar as the fourth of his Twelve Labors. This beast was associated with a deity called "Mistress of the Beasts" (*potnia theron*), who may or may not have been an aspect of the wild goddess Artemis. In another myth Artemis sent a wild boar to kill the mortal Adonis, who had bragged that he was as good a hunter as she was.

The list of heroes who took part in the hunt is too long to name them all. The more prominent names include Atalanta, the famous huntress and athlete; Castor and Pollux, semidivine twins associated with the constellation of Gemini; Jason; Deucalion the son of Minos (suggesting a time before Theseus went to Crete, although he is named in only one source and his inclusion on the list is regarded as unreliable); Laertes the father of Odysseus (suggesting

The hunt for the Calydonian Boar, on a second-century AD sarcophagus in the Archeological Museum of Piraeus. Theseus and Pirithous played a minor role in this tale. (Giovanni Dall'Orto)

a time before the Trojan War); Nestor and Telamon, also Argonauts; and of course Theseus and Pirithous.

Several of the heroes initially refused to hunt alongside a woman, but Atalanta drew first blood with an arrow, and after many adventures and mishaps the boar was brought down by Meleager, the son of Oenus.

When Meleager offered Atalanta the skin and tusks as trophies, several of the other heroes were offended that a woman should receive the prize, and Meleager killed his brother and uncle in the ensuing quarrel. When Meleager's mother Althaea heard what had happened, she caused his death by throwing a log on to the fire; at Meleager's birth the Fates had told Althaea that Meleager would live only until this brand had burned down, whereupon she had taken it from the hearth and kept it in a chest for his whole life.

Theseus and Pirithous played only a minor role in the hunt, and did not cover themselves with glory. According to the Roman poet Ovid, Theseus' spear hit a tree-branch instead of the boar, while Pirithous is mentioned only in the initial list of the hunters.

The Seven Against Thebes

Thebes (not to be confused with the ancient Egyptian capital of the same name) is a smaller city to the northwest of Athens. It is most famous for its role in the story of Oedipus, who ruled the city before his tragic downfall.

The story of *The Seven Against Thebes* tells of a dispute between Oedipus' two sons over who should rule the city. Polynices, dispossessed by his brother Eteocles, raises an army and attacks the city, and the two brothers kill each other in battle.

Theseus does not appear in the famous tragedy by the Athenian writer Aeschylus, but both Pausanias and Pseudo-Apollodorus state that after the battle he helped to ensure that the fallen received proper burial. This brief appearance mirrors his role in Sophocles' tragedy *Oedipus at Colonus*, which is not backed up by historical sources.

The Death of Theseus

The island of Skyros is roughly in the middle of the Aegean Sea, between the modern nations of Greece and Turkey. There are two versions of the events that led Theseus there.

According to some sources, Theseus left Athens in grief after the deaths of Phaedra and Hippolytus. Plutarch, on the other hand, says that he was forced out of Athens by a political faction that had grown up there while he was trapped in the Underworld.

Whatever his reasons for leaving Athens, Theseus asked Lycomedes to grant him lands and estates on Skyros. Shortly thereafter, though, Theseus fell to his death from a cliff. Some say that Lycomedes pushed Theseus off the cliff while the two were out surveying the island to find a place for Theseus to settle, either because he feared that Theseus' prestige and popularity would threaten

his own rule or because he wanted to curry favor with Theseus' opponents in Athens. Others say that Theseus fell accidentally during an after-dinner stroll.

Theseus' Tomb

Remarkably, Plutarch reports that Theseus was all but forgotten in Athens after his death. Almost a thousand years later, at the Battle of Marathon in 490 BC, Theseus' ghost appeared on the battlefield and led the Athenian charge against the Persian invaders. It was only after this that Theseus came to be regarded as an Athenian hero or demigod. Plutarch mentions that there were "many other things" beside this one miraculous appearance, but does not provide any details.

After the Persian War, the Oracle of Delphi told the Athenians to bring Theseus' bones back to the city and keep them with great care and honor. The Athenian commander Cimon captured Skyros and searched the island for Theseus' tomb. Plutarch reports that Cimon "chanced to behold an eagle pecking with its beak and scratching with its talons at a small rising ground. Here he dug, imagining that the spot had been pointed out by a miracle. There was found the coffin of a man of great stature, and lying beside it a brazen lance-head and a sword."

The remains were brought back to Athens with great ceremony and reburied there. Plutarch reports that even in his own day, five centuries later, the people of Athens sacrificed and held ceremonies in honor of Theseus.

The location of Theseus' tomb is unclear. Plutarch states that it was "near where the Gymnasium now stands," which would place it a little way north of the Agora or marketplace. To the west of the Agora, and some 200 yards away from the Gymnasium, stands the Hephaisteion, a temple to the smith-god Hephaestus, which has also been thought of as the site of Theseus' tomb. An alternative name for the temple is the Theseion, and it is covered with reliefs showing scenes from the hero's life. Based on inscriptions, though, it seems that the Hephaisteion is firmly associated with Hephaestus.

Theseus' Descendants

Theseus had four children – all sons – whose descent is not disputed: Melanippus, Hippolytus, Demophon, and Acamas. Staphylus and Oenopion were the sons of Ariadne, but their names suggest that their father was her second husband Dionysus. Some online sources refer to "a girl named Haploids and a boy named Adrift" but no primary sources can be found for these two names. Haploids is a term used in the science of genetics, and Adrift is not a Greek name-form.

Melanippus

Melanippus was Theseus' son by Perigune, the daughter of Sinis the Pine Bender. He does not play any role in recorded history or mythology, but his son (Theseus' grandson) Ioxus established a Greek colony in Caria (southwestern Anatolia in modern Turkey) and founded a family known as the Ioxides. Caria remained culturally Greek throughout Classical times and was later a province of the Byzantine Empire.

Hippolytus

Hippolytus was Theseus' son by his Amazon wife. Some sources name her as Hippolyta, the queen of the Amazons, while others state that she was an Amazon warrior named Antiope. Hippolytus grew up to be a devout follower of Artemis, sworn to chastity. When he rejected the amorous advances of his stepmother Phaedra, he set in motion a chain of events that ended both their lives and became a favorite subject for tragic playwrights.

Demophon and Acamas

Theseus had two sons by Phaedra, named Demophon (also called Demophon of Athens to distinguish him from others of the same name) and Acamas. Some sources claim that Demophon's mother was not Phaedra but Iope. Iope was the daughter of Iphicles, the wholly mortal half-brother of Hercules. In either case, Theseus is named as his father.

After Theseus was exiled from Athens, Demophon and Acamas went to Euboea, a large island to the north of Attica, where they grew up and became allies of the island's King Elephenor. The brothers both fought in the Trojan War, although Homer does not mention them (but, confusingly, the *Iliad* does mention a Trojan warrior named Acamas). Later sources name Demophon and Acamas among the Greek warriors who hid inside the Trojan Horse. In the ravaged city of Troy they found their grandmother Aethra; Castor and Pollux had taken her from Athens as Helen's maid when they rescued their kidnapped sister, and she had later accompanied the princess to Troy.

On the way home from the war, Demophon married a Thracian princess named Phyllis, but he left for Athens the day after the wedding, promising to return. Phyllis gave him a casket and made him promise not to open it unless he had lost all hope of returning to Thrace. Demophon eventually settled in Cyprus and forgot all about his wife, who finally hanged herself out of despair when he failed to return. Some time later, Demophon found the casket, which he had also forgotten, and opened it out of curiosity. What he found inside is not recorded, but apparently it was horrifying. He jumped on his horse and rode away furiously until he fell from the saddle and landed fatally on his own sword.

An alternate version of the tale recounts that Demophon did return to Thrace, only to find Phyllis dead and magically transformed into an almond tree. When the grieving Demophon embraced the tree, it miraculously blossomed.

The Greek playwright Euripides ignores these myths and has Demophon succeed his father as king of Athens. In his play *Heracleidae ("Children of Heracles")*, Demophon grants the children of Hercules refuge in Athens from their pursuit by King Eurystheus of Tiryns.

Acamas fell in love with Laodice, the daughter of King Priam of Troy, before the war when he visited the city as part of a diplomatic mission to try to recover Helen peacefully. The couple had a son called Munitus, who was raised in Priam's palace by Acamas' grandmother Aethra. Nothing else is said of Munitus, and little else is known of Acamas except that he died of a snakebite while hunting in Thrace.

THE LEGEND GROWS

The adventures of Theseus have been popular subjects for artists and writers from Classical times to the present day. This chapter presents a brief summary of the most significant works.

The Ancient World

Theseus appears on Greek reliefs and painted vases dating from the sixth century BC onward, and on Roman mosaics from Pompeii and elsewhere. These and other depictions can be found throughout this book.

Theseus appears in minor roles in many plays from Classical Greece onward, and there were at least two lost plays about his life. However, it was the tragic story of Phaedra and Hippolytus that has provided the most successful stage adaptations of all the Theseus stories.

The Athenian playwright Sophocles wrote lost plays on both Theseus and Phaedra. (The Print Collector / Alamy)

Euripides

The fifth-century Athenian playwright Euripides wrote two plays titled *Hippolytus*, only one of which survives intact. The first, *Hippolytos Kalyptomenos* ("Hippolytus Veiled," now lost) was said to have been a critical failure, probably due to Euripides' handling of Phaedra. She is depicted as brazenly propositioning her stepson. A second play, *Hippolytos Stephanophoros* ("Hippolytus Crowned"), presents Phaedra as a more complex character who struggles with her attraction to Hippolytus, the work of a jealous Aphrodite whom Hippolytus had rejected in favor of chaste Artemis.

Euripides also wrote a lost play titled *Theseus*, and Theseus is mentioned in his tragedy *Heracles*, when Hercules recounts his adventures in the Underworld.

Sophocles

A contemporary of Euripides (though some say he wrote earlier), Sophocles is best known today for his so-called Theban plays, a trilogy that tells the story of the doomed King Oedipus of Thebes. Theseus plays a role in the second play, *Oedipus at Colonus*, appearing as the king of Athens to offer refuge to Oedipus and his daughter Antigone. Sophocles also wrote plays titled *Theseus* and *Phaedra*, both of which survive only in fragments.

Ovid

The first-century Roman poet Ovid (Publius Ovidius Naso) referred to Theseus in two of his most famous works. The *Metamorphoses*, which showed Theseus and Pirithous in the hunt for the Calydonian Boar, has been mentioned. The *Heroides* ("Heroines") is a series of 15 poems that take the form of letters written by various women from Greek and Roman mythology to their lovers. Two of the poems refer to the story of Theseus.

In the fourth poem, Phaedra confesses her illicit love to Hippolytus, begging him to "acknowledge the favor I give you and conquer your hard heart." Phaedra offers Hippolytus all of Crete as her dowry and mentions Pasiphae's passion for the bull, saying "will you be more savage than that wild bull?" Although Phaedra acknowledges that her love for Hippolytus is wrong, she confesses that she is helpless before her passion.

The tenth poem is addressed by Ariadne to Theseus after he has abandoned her on Naxos. She expresses her dismay at his abandonment and wishes that she had never helped Theseus defeat the Minotaur, begging Theseus to come back for her.

Seneca

Phaedra, by the first-century Roman writer Seneca the Younger, is thought to draw upon Sophocles' lost play as well as other sources, including the lost Greek playwright Lycophron and the poetry of Ovid.

Theseus is missing in the Underworld, and it seems that he may never return. Phaedra is once again a slave to her passions rather than the unlucky victim of divine jealousy. Instead of committing suicide before Hippolytus' death, Phaedra lives long enough to berate Theseus for cursing his son, reveal her deception, and fall upon a sword.

A modern adaptation of Seneca's play, *Phaedra's Love* by British playwright Sarah Kane, was first performed in 1996 at London's Gate Theatre. This version focuses on Hippolytus, making him lazy and cynical rather than unbendingly moral.

The Minotaur seen by Virgil and Dante in Hell by Gustave Doré.

Later Retellings

Historians agree that we will never know how much Classical science and literature were lost following the collapse of the Roman Empire. From the Middle Ages onward, writers took pieces of the Theseus myth from the surviving Classical sources and adapted it for their own times.

Boccaccio, Chaucer, and Shakespeare

The 14th-century Florentine poet Giovanni Boccaccio is best known for his *Decameron*, a collection of tales illustrating life in Renaissance Italy. He also wrote a 12-book epic poem titled *Teseida delle Nozze d'Emilia* ("The Theseid, Concerning the Nuptials of Emilia"). Although the poem's stated subject is the life and career of Theseus, the main narrative concerns the rivalry between two cousins, Palemone and Arcita, for the love of Emilia, who is the younger sister of the Amazon queen Hippolyta.

Chaucer used the same story in *The Knight's Tale,* the first of his renowned *Canterbury Tales,* and Shakespeare (now agreed to have been working with John Fletcher) also used it in his late play *The Two Noble Kinsmen.*

Theseus also appears, as a fairly minor character, in Shakespeare's better-known play *A Midsummer Night's Dream*, which is set around his wedding to Hippolyta.

Dante

In Book 9 of the *Inferno*, Dante refers to the adventures of Theseus and Pirithous in the Underworld, listing them among the mortals who have come this way before. Dante and Virgil encounter the Furies, who mention how they spared Theseus and threaten to summon Medusa to turn the poet to stone. Pirithous, who remained in the Underworld, is neither seen nor mentioned.

Jean Racine

Jean Racine (1639–99) was a contemporary of Molière and is regarded today as one of France's greatest tragic playwrights. He had written plays on several Classical subjects before he turned to Phaedra in 1677.

Racine's plot is more complex than those of his predecessors. Theseus is missing and presumed dead. Phaedra is under pressure to secure the succession to the throne of Athens by forming an alliance with his son Hippolytus. This would allow her to declare the secret and obsessive love she has long held for her stepson, which has slowly driven her to the brink of hysteria. Hippolytus, far from being a cold, chaste devotee of Artemis, is secretly in love with a princess from a dynasty that Theseus supplanted, who has been placed under a vow of chastity against her will.

Phaedra tries to sabotage their love, but without success. She obtains Hippolytus' sword and when Theseus unexpectedly returns, its presence in her chamber is claimed as evidence of rape. Theseus banishes Hippolytus, who flees to the side of his princess. Theseus, witnessing their tenderness, begins to doubt his son's guilt, but is too late to prevent the curse from taking its fatal effect. Phaedra confesses all before taking poison, and a remorseful Theseus adopts his dead son's beloved as his own daughter.

The 20th Century

After Racine, there were few significant retellings of the Theseus myth in English until the middle of the 20th century, although the subject continued to be popular with artists and sculptors, as will be seem from many of the illustrations in this book.

Literary Retellings

Mary Renault's *The King Must Die* (1958) and its sequel *The Bull from the Sea* (1962) remain in print today. Renault retells the myth in a very matter-of-fact style, setting it in a realistic version of the Bronze Age Mediterranean with all of the myth's fantastic elements explained. Thus, for example, the sacrifice to the Minotaur is actually the famed Cretan bull-dance, the Minotaur itself is a man wearing a ritual mask, and the Centaurs are a wholly human tribe who live very closely with their horses. Like Renault's books on Alexander the Great, Socrates, and Plato, this is very well-researched and well-reasoned historical fiction. The first volume covers Theseus' career up to his return to Athens, while the second follows his friendship with Pirithous, his relationship with Hippolyta, and his marriage to Phaedra.

"Tribute to the Minotaur," from an American political cartoon (Library of Congress)

Several other retellings have followed Renault's, both literary and cinematic. Steven Pressfield's *Last of the Amazons* (2002) focuses on the conflict between the growing Greek civilization and the steppe-dwelling Amazon horse-clans. The book was optioned by Hollywood director James Cameron, but no movie version has yet appeared. British actor and TV presenter Tony Robinson, best known as Baldrick in the *Blackadder* series, wrote a children's retelling of the Minotaur story with *Blackadder* co-creator Richard Curtis in 1998, under the title *Theseus – The King Who Killed the Minotaur*.

One of the most interesting 20th-century adaptations of the myth was "The House of Asterion," a short story by famous Argentinean writer Jorge Luis Borges, which was first published in 1947. Borges gives the Minotaur's point of view, depicting him as isolated and longing for a "redeemer" who will free him from his life.

The myth of Theseus and the Minotaur continues to inspire modern writers. Suzanne Collins, the author of the best-selling *Hunger Games* trilogy, is quoted as saying that the story of Minos' demand for Athenian children as hostages, combined with the images of Roman gladiatorial games and modern reality television, gave her the initial idea for the series. The Minotaur also appears in the book and movie versions of Rick Riordan's *Percy Jackson and the Lightning Thief*, where it is slain by the eponymous hero.

Movies and Television

One of the earliest movie versions of the story was *Teseo contro il minotauro* ("Theseus vs. the Minotaur"), a low-budget Italian movie released in 1960 and available in English under the titles *Warlord of Crete* and *Minotaur: Wild Beast of Crete*. Directed by Silvio Amadio and starring American actor and former athlete Bob Mathias as Theseus, the film was standard Italian sword-and-sandal fare, comparable to the Steve Reeves *Hercules* movies that were popular at that time.

However, this was not the first movie treatment of Theseus. A 1910 Vitagraph silent picture titled *The Minotaur* is now apparently lost, but the *Gettysburg Times* of September 21 that year mentions a showing at the town's Walter Theater. The paper's plot summary, which was printed entirely without punctuation, reads "Theseus a young Greek brought up in obscurity by his mother proves his strength and departs for Athens to meet his father the king."

The Minotaur was seen very infrequently between 1960 and 1990. Donald Pleasance and Peter Cushing starred in the 1976 movie *The Devil's Men*, which featured a Minotaur cult kidnapping young women for sacrifice. The same year, the *Scooby-Doo* gang defeated it in an episode titled *Lock the Door, It's a Minotaur!* A similar encounter took place in 1983 in the episode *Scooby and the Minotaur*. In 1979, the legend served as the basis for the *Doctor Who* serial, *The Horns of the Nimon*, the Nimon themselves being giant humanoids with bull heads.

Henry Cavill as Theseus in the 2011 film *Immortals*. (AF archive / Alamy)

The advent of computer-generated visual effects gave the Minotaur a new lease of life on screen. Between 1990 and 2013, the Internet Movie Database (imdb.com) lists more than 20 movies and TV episodes featuring Theseus, the Minotaur, or both. The Minotaur faces a bewildering array of foes including Sinbad (three times), Hercules (both the Disney and Kevin Sorbo versions), the Beastmaster, modern teens who happen to be descended from Greek gods, and even a band of misfit toys called the Raggy Dolls.

Theseus' kidnapping of Helen is retold in the 2003 miniseries *Helen of Troy*; in this version, Theseus is killed by Pollux and Helen is returned to Sparta. Theseus also appears in the 2011 movie *Immortals*, which rewrites the myth to include the evil King Hyperion of Heraklion (a modern Cretan city close to the site of Knossos) who is searching for a powerful divine weapon that he intends to use against the gods. Phaedra is featured as a virgin prophetess who assists Theseus and eventually falls in love with him; the Minotaur is one of Hyperion's minions and is slain by Theseus. The sought-after weapon is found embedded in a rock, echoing Theseus' recovery of his father's sword.

A movie titled *Theseus* is said to be in production and scheduled for a 2014 release, but no further details were available at the time of writing.

Games

Since the first edition of *Dungeons & Dragons* was published in 1974, Minotaurs (usually treated as a race rather than a single, unique creature) have been a common foe in fantasy games. Most games treat them as little more than bull-headed ogres; their origins are seldom explained, beyond rumors of vengeful or bestial deities. In Games Workshop's *Warhammer* fantasy setting, Minotaurs are larger and more powerful versions of the goat-like Beastmen whose bodies have been warped by the Ruinous Powers of Chaos.

Minotaurs receive a very similar treatment in most video games. They tend to be a mid-ranking enemy with great strength and toughness but only average intelligence. Where Minotaur culture is portrayed, it tends to be a warrior society similar to those of fantasy barbarians, where status is based almost entirely on fighting prowess.

Like tabletop fantasy games, most video games do not show Minotaurs in their legendary context. One interesting exception is Sony's *God of War* series, which is set in a world inspired by Greek myth. Although they are a race rather than a unique creature, the Minotaurs favor axes, recalling the other major symbol of Minoan culture. The series features many different breeds of Minotaurs, with varying strengths and special powers. In *God of War II* (2007), the game's hero Kratos fights a duel with Theseus to determine who is the greatest warrior in all Greece.

In *God of War III* (2010), Kratos enters the Underworld and encounters Minos, Rhadamanthys, and Aeacus (who is substituted in some myths for Minos' second brother Sarpedon) in their roles as judges of the dead. In the Underworld he comes across the imprisoned Pirithous (the game uses the alternate spelling Pierithous). Kratos also encounters Daedalus, who is imprisoned in the Labyrinth.

A great many other video games have used the imagery of the Minotaur. The massive multiplayer online roleplaying game (MMORPG) *World of Warcraft* features a Minotaur race called the Tauren, peaceful hunters who worship the Earthmother, the goddess of nature. True to their bullish appearance, they are fierce fighters when roused to anger. *World of* Warcraft's main competitor, *Everquest,* features more traditional Minotaurs who are clannish warriors following a variety of evil masters. Kabam's *Dragons of Atlantis* features Minotaur troops in both its web and mobile versions.

The Minotaur Brand

The Minotaur's powerful image has ensured it a place in popular culture. Its name can be found on products from a rugged mountain bike through a range of gun holsters to a military engineering vehicle, a sports car, a launch rocket, and an antitank mine. The name has also been adopted by American professional wrestler Steve DiSalvo and Brazilian mixed martial artist Antônio Rodrigo Nogueira.

HMS *Minotaur*. Launched in 1863, this Royal Navy ironclad was the third of six British ships to bear that name. The name HMS *Theseus* has been used only three times.

Britain's Royal Navy has had no fewer than six ships named HMS *Minotaur*. The first was a 74-gun ship of the line launched in 1793 that fought under Nelson at the Nile and Trafalgar; the most recent was a cruiser (which gave its name to a class of similar cruisers) launched in 1943. The US Navy's USS *Minotaur* served in World War II and Korea as a specialized vessel for the repair of landing craft.

Theseus has given his name to three Royal Navy ships. One, like the first HMS *Minotaur*, was a 74-gun ship of the line and served at the Battle of the Nile. The second, launched in 1892, was a cruiser that served in World War I. The third and last HMS *Theseus* was a light aircraft carrier launched in 1944, which went on to serve in the Korean War and the Suez crisis of 1956 before being scrapped in 1962. The Bristol Theseus turboprop engine was tested in 1947 but was never developed commercially, being superseded by the more powerful Proteus.

On this evidence, the Minotaur seems to have won the battle of the brands quite decisively. Theseus is known as the hero who slew the Minotaur, but the Minotaur is much more than just another of Theseus' foes. It has spawned whole fantasy races, and moved on to more famous opponents such as Hercules and Sinbad.

CONCLUSION

While Theseus had the mix of divine and royal blood that all Greek heroes required, it might be argued that there is little that sets him apart from the others. Although he began his heroic career by lifting a great stone, he was not as strong as Hercules. Although he tricked Periphetes out of his club, he was not as cunning as Odysseus. Although he overcame many enemies in battle, he was not as invincible as Achilles. When he ventured into the Underworld, it was for a baser reason than Orpheus. And although his later life was marked by tragedy, he was not as extravagantly doomed as Oedipus.

Even though Theseus overcame many dangerous foes in his career, they were almost always more colorful than he was. The bandits he encountered on the road to Athens were memorable, each with his own particular form of murder, like prototype supervillains. The Minotaur, whose killing marked the pinnacle of Theseus' career, was – and remains – a truly iconic monster.

A Minotaur from the 2005 film *The Chronicles of Narnia: The Lion, The Witch and the Wardrobe.* (AF archive / Alamy)

Even Theseus' acts as king of Athens tell us little about his personality. Although Plutarch writes about his social and political reforms in great detail, they seem like little more than the mythic retrofitting of the necessary steps for creating a democratic regional power. Of all the tales of Theseus, this is the most obvious Athenian propaganda, invoking the memory of the city's great hero to add luster to the political and social principles that the city espoused.

Yet it is still possible to reconstruct something of Theseus the man by a careful reading of the myths. Setting aside thoughts of his myth as an allegory constructed by later Athenians and taking the hero himself at face value, Theseus emerges as a vivid and very human character.

His early adventures show a young man who is aware of the responsibilities of a hero. He makes a vital land route safe for travelers, removes a menace from the plain of Marathon, and leads the defense of his father's city against a dangerous and cunning foe. This sense of responsibility also shows in his willingness to confront the Minotaur.

Theseus' civic reforms as king of Athens show the same devotion to duty, coupled with a belief in Athens' destiny both as a regional power and as a budding democracy. When he appears in the stories of others as king of Athens, he is always shown as a just and compassionate ruler. Few kings of the time would willingly step down rather than enjoying the fruits of rulership, and while Theseus was not afraid to use his royal power, we sense that he did not use it for his own gain.

Theseus also seems to have had a considerable personal charm, which made him especially attractive to women. Had he not won Ariadne's heart he might never have found his way out of the Labyrinth, and few other heroes could have won the affections of such different women as Phaedra and Antiope. These relationships were more than mere dalliances, resulting in children whom Theseus recognized as his own legitimate issue. His abandonment of Ariadne is troubling, but many of the retellings take considerable pains to absolve him of any guilt: he was warned off by the god Dionysus on Naxos, or Ariadne died in childbirth on Cyprus, or she remained to rule Crete when Theseus was obliged to return to Athens.

Even so, Theseus seems to have had an inconstant heart, as other dalliances show. Arguably this made him no different from any other man of his times, but that is significant in itself; whatever his other virtues, Theseus was not unusually loyal in romantic matters.

Theseus' charm was not just for the ladies. He could trick Periphetes into dropping his guard, and he could even talk Minos himself into testing his divine ancestry. Although the story does not explicitly say so, Theseus must also have persuaded Minos to change the terms of his demand for Athenian hostages. Minos spared Theseus' companions from entering the Labyrinth, and his demand for a regular tribute ceased altogether after Theseus slew the Minotaur. The monster's death did nothing to atone for the death of Androgeus, yet it set Theseus and his fellow hostages free.

But Theseus was also more than just a pretty face and a silver tongue. He slew many foes, including the Minotaur, in single combat, and fought Pirithous to a standstill in their first encounter. He was also an able enough strategist and commander to rout the Sons of Pallas and – if we take the account of Cleidemus at face value – to plan and carry out a successful assault on the capital of the Eastern Mediterranean's greatest power. His skill in unarmed combat was such that he is credited with inventing the sport of wrestling, and he overcame Cercyon of Eleusis without recourse to arms, as well as – in some versions – the animal strength of the Minotaur and/or the arrogant General Taurus.

Whatever one makes of Theseus' relationship with Pirithous, their bond was a strong one. Theseus literally went to hell and back for his friend, and lamented his loss ever afterward. However, he was practical enough to accept Hercules' advice that the task of recovering Pirithous from Hades was impossible.

In an age when fantasy has surpassed mythology as a popular form of literature and Theseus has been eclipsed by the Minotaur, it is still interesting to consider the nature of this enigmatic hero. Reading between the lines of his adventures, he seems unusually modest for a Greek hero. He is dutiful and compassionate, and has a strong sense of justice. He can be charming, and knows how to use that charm when dealing with men as well as women. Although his kidnapping of a pubescent Helen seems out of keeping with his previous character, it might be seen as a desperate attempt at a last great adventure in the face of old age and the tedium of rulership. Whatever his virtues, Theseus stands among the most human of the Greek heroes.

GLOSSARY

This book contains a large number of names, not all of which will be familiar to most readers. This glossary offers brief explanations of the various characters and places that are connected with the story of Theseus, as well as the names of the most important ancient sources.

Aegeus: A legendary king of Athens and the mortal father of Theseus. The Aegean Sea is said to be named after him.

Aeschylus: An Athenian playwright of the fifth century BC, most famous for his trilogy *The Oresteia*, which told of a curse that led to the fall of Mycenae.

Aethra: The mother of Theseus. A princess of the city of Troezen in the northeastern Peloponnese.

Androgeus: A Cretan prince, the eldest son of Minos and Pasiphae, whose death led to Minos demanding a regular sacrifice of seven youths and seven maidens from Athens.

Antiope: An Amazon warrior, possibly the mother of Theseus' son Hippolytus.

Ariadne: A daughter of King Minos of Crete, who fell in love with Theseus and helped him defeat the Minotaur. In some versions of the myth, Theseus married her and then left her on the island of Naxos where she became the bride of Dionysus; other sources claim that this Ariadne was someone else.

Asterion: The true name of the Minotaur. Also the foster-father of Minos and his brothers.

Attica: The region of Greece surrounding Athens.

Calydonian Boar: A wild boar that terrorized the area around Calydon in western Greece. Theseus played a minor role in the hunt that killed it.

Castor and Pollux: Twin demigods, associated with the constellation Gemini. They were regarded as patrons of sailors and associated with horsemanship. Among other adventures, they sailed with Jason and the Argonauts.

Centaurs: A half-human horse-people from Greek myth. Interpreted by some writers as a mythologized form of a horse culture similar to those of the Eurasian steppes.

Cerberus: A monstrous three-headed watchdog kept by Hades.

Cercyon: A king of Eleusis whom Theseus defeated in a wrestling match on his way to Athens.

Cimon: An Athenian general of the fifth century BC, credited with bringing Theseus' remains back from Skyros to Athens.

Cleidemus: A Greek author, probably of the fifth or fourth century BC, whose work is now lost. Plutarch refers to his account that Theseus led an Athenian attack on Crete.

Crommyonian Sow: A monstrous pig killed by Theseus on his way to Athens.

Daedalus: A legendary inventor and engineer who designed the Labyrinth. He escaped from Crete using artificial wings, but his son Icarus flew too close to the sun and was killed.

Deucalion: A son of Minos, possibly the same person as the General Taurus mentioned by Plutarch.

Dionysus: The Greek god of wine, identified with the Roman Bacchus.

Elysium: Also known as the Elysian Fields. An afterworld reserved for heroes and the blessed, sometimes equated with the Christian heaven.

Euripides: A Greek playwright of the fifth century BC, renowned for his tragedies. His work includes *Hippolytus*, which tells the story of Hippolytus and Phaedra.

Furies (Greek *Erinyes*): Winged female deities whose duty is to punish evildoers.

Hades: The Greek god of the Underworld, which is sometimes named after him.

Helen: A Spartan princess and sister of the twin demigods Castor and Pollux. Theseus and Pirithous kidnapped her, provoking her brothers to attack Athens. She later became famous as Helen of Troy.

Hephaisteion: An Athenian temple to the smith-god Hephaestus and a possible site of Theseus' tomb. Also called the Theseion from its reliefs showing scenes from the hero's life.

Hippolyta: An Amazon queen, possibly the mother of Theseus' son Hippolytus.

Hippolytus: Theseus' son by an Amazon, either Hippolyta or Antiope.

Knossos: The capital of King Minos of Crete.

Labyrinth: "House of the Double Axe." An elaborate maze constructed to house the Minotaur. Alternatively, a fortress or prison near the palace of Knossos.

Lapiths: A people from the hilly country of Thessaly. Theseus' friend Pirithous was their prince, and later their king.

Lycomedes: King of the island of Skyros, where Theseus planned to retire after withdrawing from Athens. According to some accounts he murdered Theseus by throwing him off a cliff.

Marathonian Bull: A monstrous bull that terrorized the Plain of Marathon outside Athens until Theseus captured it.

Melanippus: Theseus' son by Perigune, the daughter of Sinis (q.v.).

Minoan: The late Bronze Age culture of Crete. The name was coined by British archeologist Sir Arthur Evans in the 19th century, and is taken from the name of King Minos.

Minos: The legendary ruler of Crete, a son of Zeus and the Phoenician princess Europa.

Mnestheus: A political opponent of Theseus and possible conspirator in his death.

Mycenaean: A Greek culture of the late Bronze Age, named after the site of Mycenae about 30 miles south of Corinth.

Naxos: The largest of the Cyclades islands in the Aegean Sea. Theseus visited Naxos on his way back from Crete and left Ariadne there.

Nereids: Sea nymphs from Greek mythology.

Oenopion: A son of Theseus by Ariadne. His name means "wine drinker," implying that his father might really be Dionysus, Ariadne's second husband.

Ovid (Publius Ovidius Naso): A Roman poet of the first century AD, whose works include the mythological *Metamorphoses*, published in 15 books.

Pallantides: Also known as "the 50 sons of Pallas." A faction of Attic nobles, nephews of Aegeus, who coveted the throne of Athens until Theseus defeated them.

Panathenaic Games: A successor to the Pan-Athenian Games (see below), instituted by Theseus according to some sources.

Pan-Athenian Games: Games held every four years in Athens. The Cretan prince Androgeus was killed while visiting Athens to compete.

Pasiphae: The wife of King Minos, cursed with an unnatural lust for a white bull.

Pausanias: A Greek geographer of the second century AD, whose ten-book *Description of Greece* has been described as a crucial link between classical literature and modern archeology.

Peloponnese: The part of Greece that lies south of the Isthmus of Corinth.

Perigune: The daughter of Sinis (q.v.) and mother of Theseus' son Melanippus.

Periphetes: A bandit famed for his bronze club, defeated by Theseus on his journey to Athens.

Persephone: The daughter of the harvest-goddess Demeter, kidnapped by Hades to be his bride.

Phaedra: Sister of Ariadne (q.v.) and wife of Theseus, who accused her stepson Hippolytus of raping her, with tragic consequences.

Philochorus: A Greek historian of the third century BC, whose work survives only in fragments. Plutarch cites him as claiming that the Labyrinth was a fortress rather than the lair of a monster.

Pittheus: A legendary king of Troezen. Theseus' grandfather.

Pirithous (also Perithoos, Peirithoos, or Peirithous): A prince of the Lapith people of Thessaly to the north of Attica. Theseus' companion for many of his later adventures; possibly also his lover.

Plutarch: A first-century Greek writer (*c.* 46–120 AD), famous for his biographies including the *Life of Theseus*.

Poseidon: The Greek sea-god, identified with the Roman Neptune.

Procrustes: A bandit whom Theseus defeated on his way to Athens. Procrustes forced his victims to lie on an iron bed, either stretching them or lopping off their feet until they fitted it exactly.

Pseudo-Apollodorus ("False Apollodorus"): The writer of a historical work titled *Bibliotheca* ("The Library"), which was wrongly attributed to the second-century BC historian Apollodorus of Athens.

Racine, Jean: French playwright of the 17th century. His play *Phèdre* tells the story of Phaedra and Hippolytus.

Sciron: A bandit defeated by Theseus on his way to Athens. Sciron would force passers-by to wash his feet, and kick them off a cliff when they bent to do so. Not to be confused with Skyros, the island where Theseus died.

Seneca (Lucius Annaeus Seneca): Roman Stoic philosopher and writer of the first century AD. His play *Phaedra* tells the story of Hippolytus and Phaedra.

Ship of Theseus: A philosophical paradox based on the fact that the Athenians preserved Theseus' ship, replacing parts as they decayed until nothing of the original was left.

Sinis: A bandit defeated by Theseus on his way to Athens. Sinis lashed his victims to bent pine trees whose recoil tore them apart.

Skyros: An island between Greece and Anatolia, where Theseus died. Not to be confused with Sciron, one of Theseus' early foes.

Sophocles: A Greek playwright of the fifth century BC. Theseus plays a minor role in his play *Oedipus at Colonus*, the second play in a trilogy dealing with the life of Oedipus.

Staphylus: A son of Theseus by Ariadne. His name means "grape cluster," implying that his father might really be Dionysus, Ariadne's second husband.

Tartarus: An abyss in the realm of Hades, frequently equated with the Christian hell.

Taurus: The name of a Cretan general and governor of the Labyrinth, who was defeated by Theseus in a wrestling-match. Possibly a title: Taurus may have been Minos' son Deucalion.

Thebes: A city in Greece to the northwest of Athens. Not to be confused with the famous Egyptian city of the same name.

Troezen: A city in the northeastern Peloponnese where Theseus spent his early life.

BIBLIOGRAPHY

Alighieri, Dante (trans. H. F. Carey), *The Vision of Hell*, Cassell & Co., London, 1892.

Apollodorus (trans. Robin Hard), *The Library of Greek Mythology*, Oxford University Press, Oxford, 1997.

Apollodorus and Hyginus (trans. R. Scott Smith and Stephen M. Trzaskoma), *Apollodorus' Library and Hyginus' Fabulae: Two Handbooks of Greek Mythology*, Hackett Publishing Company, Indianapolis, 2007.

Bacchylides (trans. Robert Fagles), *Complete Poems*, Yale University Press, New Haven, 1998.

Borges, Jorge Luis (trans. Andrew Hurley), "The House of Asterion," *Collected Fictions*, Penguin, New York, 1999.

Campbell, Joseph, *The Hero with a Thousand Faces*, New World Library, Novato, 2008.

Cleidemus, *Atthis*, fifth–fourth century BC, now lost.

Collins, Suzanne, *The Hunger Games*, Scholastic, New York, 2009.

Connor, Steve, "Has the original Labyrinth been found?" *The Independent*, October 16, 2009. Online version available at http://www.independent.co.uk/arts-entertainment/architecture/has-the-original-labyrinth-been-found-1803638.html

Daily Mail Reporter, "Maze of underground caves could be the original site of the ancient Greek Labyrinth," *Daily Mail*, October 16, 2009. Online version available at http://www.dailymail.co.uk/news/article-1220859/Maze-underground-caves-original-site-ancient-Greek-Labyrinth.html#ixzz1ArLrYdwN

Euripides (trans. Michael R. Halleran), *Hippolytus*, Focus Publishing/R. Pullins Co, Newburyport, MA, 2001.

Frazer, James G., *The Golden Bough*, Gramercy, New York, 1993.

Grimal, Pierre, *Larousse World Mythology*, Larousse, London, 1989.

Leeming, David, *Myth: A Biography of Belief*, Oxford University Press, Oxford, 2002.

McInerny, Jeremy, "Bulls and Bull-Leaping in the Minoan World," http://penn.museum/documents/publications/expedition/PDFs/53-3/mcinerney.pdf

Ovid (trans. Harold Isbell), *Heroides*, Penguin Classics, London, 2004.

Ovid (trans. E. J. Kenney), *Metamorphoses,* Oxford Paperbacks, Oxford, 1998.

Pausanias, *Description of Greece*, vol. I, Loeb Classical Library, Cambridge, 1918.

Plutarch (trans. Aubrey Stewart), *Plutarch's Lives*, vol. I, George Bell & Sons, London, 1894. There are many other translations, but this one is available as a free ebook on Project Gutenberg (http://www.gutenberg.org/files/14033/14033-h/14033-h.htm#LIFE_OF_THESEUS).

Pressfield, Steven, *Last of the Amazons*, Bantam, New York, 2003.

Racine, Jean (trans. Margaret Rawlings), *Phèdre*, Penguin Classics, London, 1992.

Radice, Betty, *Who's Who in the Ancient World*, Penguin Books, New York, 1971.

Renault, Mary, *The King Must Die,* Vintage, New York, 1988.

Renault, Mary, *The Bull from the Sea,* Vintage, New York, 2001.

Riordan, Rick, *Percy Jackson and the Lightning Thief*, Disney-Hyperion, New York, 2006.

Robinson, Tony and Curtis, Richard, *Theseus – The King Who Killed the Minotaur*, Hodder & Stoughton, London, 1988.

Seneca (trans. Frederick Ahl), *Phaedra*, Cornell University Press, Ithaca, NY, 1986.

Siculus, Diodorus (trans. C. H. Oldfather), *Diodorus Siculus: The Library of History*, vol. III, Loeb Classical Library,New York, 1939.

Smith, Sir William (ed.), *Dictionary of Greek and Roman Biography and Mythology*, vol. I, Little & Brown, Boston, 1849.

Movies and TV

Amadio, Silvio (dir.) *Warlord of Crete*, 1960.

Becker, Josh (dir.) *Hercules in the Maze of the Minotaur*, 1994.

English, Jonathan (dir.), *Minotaur*, 2006.

Harrison, John Kent (dir.), *Helen of Troy*, 2003.

Popplewell, Brett (prod.), "The Minotaur" (*Beastmaster*, season 1 episode 13), 2000.

Singh, Tarsem, *Immortals*, 2011.

Zwicky, Karl (dir.), *Sinbad and the Minotaur*, 2011.